COAL

BLACKWINGS
DEVIL SPRINGS

TEAGAN BROOKS

COAL

BLACKWINGS MC - DEVIL SPRINGS - BOOK 7

TEAGAN BROOKS

Adult Content Warning: For ages 18 years old and older due to graphic sexual content, explicit language, and violence.

ISBN: 978-1-951704-22-3

BLURB

Aspen

After losing my apartment and my job on the same day, I had to ask for help. There was only one person I could call, and thankfully, he came through for me. Then, an epic snowstorm hit while I was moving, leaving me stuck on the highway for fourteen hours. I thought my bad luck was over when I finally made it to Devil Springs. Little did I know, it was only just beginning.

Coal

I was on my way home when it started snowing. Traffic came to a stop and I soon found myself stuck in the middle of a snowstorm on my bike. I was beginning to think I was going to freeze to death when the woman in the moving truck next to me offered to let me sit in her truck while we waited for traffic to start moving again. I had no idea that her simple act of kindness would change my life forever.

To my readers

ACKNOWLEDGMENTS

Cover Designer: CT Cover Creations

Cover Model: Zach Fox

Cover Photographer: Golden Czermak/Furious Fotog

CHARACTER LIST

- Annabelle Black – Coal's biological mother
- Carter Perry – Pamela Perry's husband; Deceased
- Carter Perry II – Carter Perry's son; Pamela Perry's stepson
- Drew – Blackwings MC Prospect
- Edgar Romero – Lawyer; Edwin's brother
- Edwin Romero – Incarcerated drug dealer; Edgar's brother
- Ember Black Lawson – Coal's twin sister
- Game – Grant; Blackwings MC member; Coal's roommate
- Jeff Martin – Coal's adoptive father; Kathleen's husband
- Josie Cross – Tatum's sister; Works at bookstore
- Kathleen Martin – Coal's adoptive mother; Luke's sister

- Lorcan O'Shea – Sloane's father; Owns fight club in Cherryfield; Has fighters train at the Blackwings gym in Devil Springs
- Luke Johnson – FBI agent; Kathleen Martin's brother
- Mackenzie Moore – Brinkley's mother; Bear's Old Lady
- Mitzie Mayfield – Mackenzie's mother; Brinkley's grandmother; Deceased
- Pamela Perry – Carter Perry's widow; Suspect in three murders
- Phoenix Black – Coal's biological father
- Sean Perry – Carter Perry II's son; Missing
- Shane – One of Lorcan's fighters training in Devil Springs
- Sydney Gallagher – Waitress at Precious Metals

PROLOGUE

"I've been counting down the days until you were released for over a year now. Imagine how surprised I was to learn you'd been released early. Months early. Tell me, why haven't you come to see me? Were you trying to hide from me?" he sneered as he circled me.

"Because I knew why you wanted to see me. I came up with a plan, but I needed time to put it in place first."

He laughed cruelly. "And what plan is this?"

I held up my hand to show him the engagement ring on my finger. "To marry into money. I won't be able to give you everything all at once, but I'll be able to start paying you." And I'd stop as soon as I figured out another way to get him off of my back. He blamed me for his brother being sent to prison as well as for the money they lost when their little empire collapsed.

"How much are we talking? And before you say a number, I suggest you choose an amount that's more than I could make by charging people to fuck you. Because that, my dear, is my plan to recoup my losses."

Fucking bastard. There was no way I was going to

let that happen. Especially when it wasn't my fault his brother got busted. If it was anyone's fault, it was Edwin's. He's the one who insisted on coming to my house that night. He didn't like that part of my job was pretending to be in a relationship with another man. He hated it and felt the need to remark his territory the moment he could.

"Twenty thousand a month. I don't think I can do more than that without raising suspicion. And I can't start paying you until after I'm married."

Edgar stopped circling me and took a seat behind his desk. He steepled his fingers and stared at me while he considered my offer.

"Fine. You can have the rest of this month and the next. Then, I expect payment on the first. If you're late, come up short, or miss a payment, your ass is mine, and everyone else's."

* * *

Two years later

"He thinks I'm cheating on him. He cut off my access to all of his accounts," I said, hating that I was having to ask this man for help.

"That sounds like a personal problem."

"It is, but it's one I think you can help with. If you'll change his will and leave everything to me, I'll kill him and make it look like an accident."

Edgar was a lawyer. A crooked one, but a lawyer

nonetheless. He was more than capable of doing what I was asking; it was only a question of if he would.

"When you say everything. How much do you mean?"

It was always about money with him.

"A few million. More than enough to pay back what I owe you." Or what he thought I owed him.

"What if you get caught?"

I smirked. "I won't." I had it all planned out. Even if someone suspected I was behind it, there was absolutely no way they could prove it.

"I'll need a few days."

"I can't wait that long. It has to be done before he files for divorce."

"Fine," he huffed. "I'll try to have everything in order tomorrow."

"Let me know the moment you do."

* * *

Six months later

"We've got a problem," I said to the man I hated yet relied on.

"You mean you have a problem," he said and pointed to the breaking news story on the television.

"No, I mean we. That fucking PI his son hired found the original will. He also found out Carter had an appointment with a divorce attorney that was canceled the day after he died. And he put together the connection between you, me, and your brother."

"So what? None of that can be used to prove you murdered your husband."

"No, but it's more than enough to contest the will."

"Is that why you killed him?"

"Of course it is! What else was I supposed to do?"

"Offer him more money than Carter did," he said simply.

"Really? So he could take the money and give the evidence to Carter anyway? Or so he could blackmail me for the rest of my life? I don't think so."

"At the very least, you should've disposed of the bodies somewhere other than your own property."

"I only killed him. I had nothing to do with the other one." Though I couldn't say I was very upset about her death. She knew too much and was starting to become problematic. I'd considered getting rid of her and probably would have gone through with it eventually, but someone else beat me to it.

"So, why are you really here?"

"I need a place to lay low until this blows over."

"I might have somewhere for you to stay, but you're going to work while you're there."

"Doing what?"

"Packing and shipping orders," he said with a sly smile.

And just like that, I was right back where I started.

1

ASPEN

Shit. Fuck. Damn. Piss. Hell.

Son of a motherfucker.

I was beyond screwed. So far beyond screwed words couldn't begin to describe the depths of my screwedness.

I was also frustrated. And pissed. Which resulted in angry tears. And I fucking hated angry tears.

Mostly because once they started, I couldn't get them stopped until my face was an unhealthy shade of red and covered with a mixture of snot and tears.

I sighed and wiped my face again.

There was one person I could call. He made sure to tell me that the last time I saw him in person and every time I'd spoken to him on the phone since then.

"Call me if you ever need anything."

I knew he meant it.

Even though I wondered why he kept up with me, I never asked him. And if I was being honest with myself, I was afraid to ask.

Regardless, I was glad that he had. Because I was about to take him up on his offer. He was my last hope, and I had no idea what I would do if he couldn't help me.

It had been a few months since the last time I'd talked to him. And that was no one's fault but my own. I couldn't explain it, but it felt weird that one of my mother's many ex-boyfriends was the closest thing I had to a father figure in my life.

The few years he and my mother were together were the most stable of my entire existence. I didn't have the words to describe what that felt like, but it wasn't pleasant. To know that someone who was once a complete stranger cared more about you than your own family was a feeling no child should experience. And if I ever had my own children, I would cherish them, and make sure they knew how much I loved them. In other words, I would do everything the polar opposite of the way my mother had raised me.

At first, he called frequently, and I usually answered. Over time, I didn't pick up as often for various reasons, but we did talk every few months. It was hard actively avoiding him, but it was even harder to engage. Because it hurt. A lot. How could this man who hardly knew me and wasn't related to me care about me more than my own mother did? And what would happen when he found a family of his own? Because he would. He was a good man just waiting for the right woman to come along. And I didn't think I'd survive being thrown to the wayside again.

"Hey, Aspen," he answered immediately, not sounding the least bit surprised. Instead, he actually sounded like he was expecting a call from me, which completely threw me off track.

"Uh, hey," I stumbled over my words as a million thoughts raced through my mind.

Why was he expecting a call from me? What happened?

"I'm sorry. I've been meaning to call you, but things have been really busy. I'm guessing you heard about your mom."

The mere mention of my mother made the unease in my stomach churn. I didn't think I could handle news about my mother on what was already shaping up to be the worst day of my life. But I'd already learned that it was better to know sooner rather than later when it came to her.

"Mother," I corrected as I cleared my throat. "I don't have a 'mom.' And no, I haven't."

"Oh," he exhaled slowly. "I assumed that's why you were calling when I saw your name on the screen."

"It's not, but go ahead and tell me what I need to know," I said and tried to brace myself for whatever he was going to say.

I hadn't spoken to my mother in years. Since the one and only time I went to visit her after everything came to a head. When I walked out of the room they were holding her in, she was as dead to me as I was to her.

I shuddered, remembering her last words to me. *"I'm not sure what made you think I'd want to see your face, let alone breathe the same air as you, but let me clear things up for you. If I could get my hands on you right now, I'd wrap them around your neck and squeeze until there's nothing left of you."*

I tried not to let her words affect me, but how could they not? She was my mother, and was very clearly a bad person.

After I moved out and got my own place, I spent the first year scared to death and constantly looking over my shoulder, even though I knew she was behind bars. It took time, but I finally settled into some semblance of a normal life and did my best to forget about her.

"You really haven't kept up with her," he said, sounding surprised and a little proud.

That was true. I hadn't. The only way I could deal with the aftermath was to carry on like she didn't exist. If anyone asked about my family, I told them my father was never in the picture and my mother was dead. It was a mixture of the truth and what I wished was the truth. I knew it wasn't the healthiest option, but it worked for me.

"No, but you're making it sound like I should have."

I heard him sigh, and I could picture him dropping his head and pinching the bridge of his nose while holding the phone to his ear. "There's a lot more to it, but here's the short version. Her husband was found dead on her property a few months ago. It was originally ruled an accidental drowning, but the case has been reopened and is being investigated as a homicide."

"Her husband?" I almost shouted.

"Yeah, she got married not long after she was released."

"Huh," I started, unsure of what to say. The news of her release didn't surprise me. Not really. I knew how many years she'd been sentenced to, as well as when she was eligible for release, and those years had passed. I didn't care that she had gotten married, or that I had a stepfather I never knew about. I really didn't care about her at all. And I certainly didn't want him to think I did. "I never thought about what she'd do once she got out, but getting married definitely wouldn't have been on the list."

"I know, right?" he laughed.

For as long as I could remember, she'd been very vocal on her feelings regarding marriage. *"It's a one-way ticket to letting someone else take everything you've worked for."*

Even though I didn't know about my mother's marriage, it didn't have anything to do with me, so it couldn't be the reason why he thought I was calling. "What else?"

"She's a suspect in the murder."

"Why? Was he rich?" I joked.

"Yes, he was what some would consider wealthy."

"Oh," I said, suddenly uncomfortable. "I was kidding."

"There's more."

"What else could there be?" I didn't realize I'd asked it out loud until he answered.

"Her stepson was arrested for possession and manufacturing of child pornography. He has adamantly denied the charges from the moment of his arrest. He's given us a list of people who could possibly clear his name, but so far, each one has turned up either dead or missing."

"So, you're telling me my birth giver has advanced from a side-piece informant to murdering multiple people since her short stint in prison?"

"Officially? No. Unofficially? Yes."

"What does any of this have to do with me?" I asked and hoped he didn't mistake my directness for being rude. But I shouldn't have worried. If anyone understood the way I felt about my mother, he did.

"I suppose nothing. I assumed you'd gotten wind of the case and were calling to talk about it."

I wished that was why I was calling. But I had a big

problem that was only going to get bigger if I didn't find a solution in the next few hours.

"Nope. This is the first thing I've heard about her in years."

As soon as the words were out of my mouth, his entire demeanor changed. "What's wrong?"

"Why do you think something's wrong?" I asked, trying to buy myself a few seconds. I was prepared to start my spiel when he first answered the phone, but most of my bravado disappeared while we were talking about my mother.

"Because you never call. And you just used the oldest stalling trick in the book. What's going on, Aspen?" he demanded.

"Uh, well, I was supposed to move into a new apartment tomorrow, but there's a problem, and I don't know what to do."

"Tell me the problem, and we'll fix it." Just like that. I wanted to bask in his confidence and comfort. And wished I had the right to.

"There was a mix up with the paperwork, and the new apartment was leased to someone else. They don't have another one available until next month, and my current place has already been rented as well."

"It's their mistake. You're a current resident. If they gave your new apartment away, they need to let you keep the one you're in until they rectify the mistake. Do you want me to make a call?"

"That might've worked, but it's not the same complex."

"Neither place has any availability?" he asked in disbelief.

"Nothing for a few weeks. No one does.

Apparently, we're experiencing unprecedented growth." Not that it mattered much since it was going to take a few days for my security deposit to be returned, and what little savings I had left over wasn't anything to brag about.

"When do you have to be out of your place?"

"I'm supposed to turn the keys in by Monday morning."

"Damn. They sure didn't give you much time."

"At least I figured it out today instead of tomorrow," I said, repeating the same thing I'd been telling myself in a weak attempt to stay positive.

"You figured it out?"

"Yes," I said and tried to hold back the tears threatening to return. "I called to see when I could pick up the keys to the new apartment, and after a good bit of back and forth, they told me my application had been withdrawn and the apartment had already been given to someone else. They tried to help, but there wasn't anything they could do."

"Well, shit, Aspen. I know it's probably not what you were hoping for, but the house in Devil Springs is just sitting there. You're more than welcome to stay there. Always have been."

The house in Devil Springs he was referring to was the house he and my mother shared for the few years they were together. It was the house we were living in when she was arrested for the charges that ultimately put her in prison. Originally, it was a rental property, but he bought it after my mother's arrest so that I wouldn't also lose my home while the rest of my life was being flipped upside down. He'd done a lot of other things for me over the years, but buying the house for my stability showed me he was more of a parent to me than my own mother was.

"You obviously won't be able to keep your job, but I'm sure you can find something in Devil Springs. Unless you're planning on moving back to Cherryfield when an apartment becomes available."

"No worries there. I got fired when I went in for my shift tonight."

"*You* got fired? How?" he asked in disbelief.

It shocked me too. During the two years I worked at Schroder's Pub, I'd never missed a day of work, never been late, and had zero customer complaints.

"I called my boss earlier today to explain my situation and asked if I could have the night off. Dickhead Darren said no, so I asked if I could come in an hour or two late since it wasn't usually busy at the beginning of the shift. He said, 'No. I'll see you at the regular time.' I left for work like I usually did, but for the first time since I started working there, I was late. Fifteen minutes. He didn't even give me a chance to explain before he pointed to the door and told me to leave. So, I turned around and came back home to keep working on my living situation."

"You don't sound too upset about it," he said carefully.

"I'm not," I said honestly. "Darren is a relatively new manager, and I really haven't been happy there since he started."

I'm not sure what his problem was, but he seemed to dislike me immediately. He wasn't outwardly mean, but he wasn't friendly either. He was flat—his voice, his affect, his everything. And it wasn't just me. He treated all the employees the same. While it was nothing to legitimately complain about, it didn't make for the greatest of working environments.

"Anything I need to know about?" he asked, sounding like an overprotective father.

"No, nothing like that," I reassured him.

"Well, there's a silver lining. You can take the time you need to find a job you like since you won't have to worry about rent and utilities."

"If I'm going to stay there, I want to pay rent and utilities."

"Aspen, I'm going to be honest with you. Your mother is wanted for questioning regarding her involvement in three murders as well as a list of other charges. And we can't find her. Having you here in Devil Springs will give me a peace of mind I wouldn't have otherwise. In exchange for that, I'll take care of the bills."

I knew there was no point in arguing with him. Besides, I didn't have the money to pay for anything anyway. I barely had enough to cover groceries and other necessities after paying for the moving truck.

"I'll agree on one condition."

"Let's hear it."

"You let me pay rent once she's caught."

"Does that mean you're taking my offer?" he asked hopefully.

I exhaled slowly. "Yes, I am. Thank you."

"You don't have to thank me. I never wanted you to leave in the first place," he said and cleared his throat. "Do you still have a key to the house?"

"Yes, I do," I said as I looked at the key that was still on my key ring. Even though I'd never planned on going back, I held onto the key for some reason, and it was a good thing I did.

"Good. If you want, I can have someone come by and change the locks once you're settled in. I did have an alarm system installed after you moved out. 'Your bday' is the code."

"Did you just say 'bday?'"

"Yes. The code is eight digits. 'Your bday.' Spell it out on the keypad," he explained.

"How did you come up with that?"

He chuckled. "Everyone says not to use your birthday for passwords. You know how much I love a good play on words."

"You sure do," I laughed. He was a self-proclaimed word nerd. His words, not mine. I'd secretly been fascinated by his word games as a teenager.

"All right, what else do I need to tell you? You'll need to make a grocery run or pick up something to eat. If there's any food in the house, I can assure you it's not edible. And the house will likely need to be aired out and dusted. I think there's a vacuum in the hall closet."

"I thought you lived there."

"Technically, I do," he said, hesitating before he continued, "but you know how my job is. When I'm gone for weeks or months at a time and only home for two or three days, the last thing I want to do is refresh a house that's been closed up for months. It's easier to stay in a hotel room for a few days."

"I'll be there by myself?" I asked, hoping I didn't sound as unsure as I felt.

"Yeah," he paused. "Is that okay?"

"Of course," I said. "I didn't realize you wouldn't be

there, but now I feel a little less guilty about crashing at your place with little to no notice."

"My place is your place. Always will be. But you're on your own moving in. I won't be back in town until sometime next week at the earliest."

"I've already loaded the moving truck by myself. Unloading it won't be any different," I said. He didn't need to know about the hell I'd gone through trying to get my mattress and sofa loaded onto the truck. I'd been able to disassemble everything and carry it to the truck one piece at a time. Everything except those two items, and I'd seriously considered leaving them behind at one point. But that would result in additional fees I didn't have the funds to pay. Plus, I needed a bed and wouldn't be able to afford a decent one until I found a new job and had worked enough to have a few paychecks under my belt.

"You sure? I can arrange to have someone meet you there to help with the heavy lifting," he offered.

But I didn't want anyone else to witness my move of shame unless they absolutely had to. He was already giving me a place to live, for free. I didn't feel right taking any more handouts from him.

"I'm sure," I said and tried to swallow past the emotion starting to clog my throat. "Thank you."

2

COAL

"Fuck," I cursed when the slowly moving traffic came to a complete stop.

According to the forecast, a winter storm was headed toward Devil Springs that was expected to drop several inches of snow, and I was trying to get home before it started. Unfortunately, I still had at least two hours to go.

I was hoping we would get moving again after a few minutes, but when snow flurries started falling from the sky, I had a feeling I was in for a long night.

"Yo! What's good?" my roommate and club brother said into the phone by way of greeting.

"Not much. I'm sitting at a standstill on the highway near Rockwood, and it just started snowing."

"Shit. Is there a wreck or something?"

"I can't see anything except the cars ahead of me, but there has to be. I've made it two miles in the last thirty minutes."

"That sucks, dude. What are you gonna do?"

"Nothing I can do but sit here and try not to freeze to death."

"You're on your bike, man. Split lanes and get out of there."

I snorted. "You think I'd still be sitting here if that was a possibility?"

"I'd hope not."

"I'm in between towns. Even if I could get off the highway, there's nowhere to go. According to my phone, the closest gas station is eight miles away."

"You can't sit on your bike all night in the snow."

"Who said anything about all night?"

"You're at a standstill on the highway, and it just started snowing. Things are probably going to get worse before they get better."

He was right. I knew it, but I wasn't ready to acknowledge my fate yet.

I sighed and moved my hand to pinch the bridge of my nose and felt like an idiot when my fingers smacked against the faceplate of my helmet. "I'll be fine," I said, not sure which one of us I was attempting to reassure. But as the snow fell harder, I realized it was me that needed convincing.

An hour later, things were much worse. The traffic hadn't moved an inch, but that was about how much snow had already accumulated on the ground. Thankfully, I had an eighteen-wheeler and a box truck on either side of me to help block some of the wind. But it was still cold. Really fucking cold.

"Yoo-hoo," a female voice called.

I glanced around and didn't see anyone. I briefly wondered if hearing voices was a sign of hypothermia, but then I heard it again and knew it was directed at me.

"Up here, Mr. Biker Man."

I glanced up to find big, green eyes peering down at me from the passenger window of the box truck next to me.

"You're going to freeze to death out there. Do you want to wait in here where it's warm?" she said and pushed the door open.

I didn't hesitate. It was so cold I was pretty sure my balls were frozen. I was off my bike and inside the warmth of her truck in the blink of an eye.

After I closed the door behind me, I pulled off my helmet and one glove. "Thank you," I said and extended my hand. "I'm Coal."

"I know; that's why I offered you a place to get warm."

I grinned and shook my head. "I am cold, but my name is Coal, like the stuff Santa gives naughty kids for Christmas."

When her eyes flicked to my outstretched hand, she placed one hand in mine and covered her face with the other. "Hi, Coal. I'm Aspen."

"Well, Aspen, what took you so long?" I teased, reluctantly letting go of her soft, warm hand.

She laughed nervously as her cheeks slightly flushed. "I'm sorry. I thought we'd be moving sooner."

"Do you know what's going on?"

"It started with a wreck, and then another one behind it. And now it's snowing."

"Yeah, I was trying to get home before the snow started."

"Do you have far to go?"

I shrugged. "About two hours, give or take. What about you?"

"Same. About two hours left."

"Let me guess. You're headed to Devil Springs?"

"How'd you know?" she gasped in surprise.

"Because there's not much else between here and there," I chuckled.

She sighed and tilted her head back toward the ceiling. "I keep looking at the clock. I should already be there unloading this truck, instead of sitting on the highway doing absolutely nothing but wasting time."

"Are you on a time crunch?"

"Sort of. I'm supposed to return this truck tomorrow, but it doesn't look like that's happening."

"Well, I, for one, am glad you're stuck here. Otherwise, my options were freezing to death or hoping that trucker over there would take pity on me. And he doesn't look nearly as friendly as you do."

She leaned forward and looked at the truck idling beside my bike. As if on cue, the driver turned his head and glared at both of us, causing her to flinch back. "He's not a helper."

"What?"

"My stepfather told me to always look for the helpers, especially in times of need. He's not one."

"My uncle used to say something like that when I was little," I said.

My phone lit up with Game's name on the screen. "You still on the highway?" he asked before I could say a word.

"Yep. In almost the same place since the last time I talked to you."

"This shit's on the news. There are so many wrecks that traffic's at a standstill and backed up for over twenty miles. They're saying motorists will likely be stranded until morning."

"Until morning? There's no fucking way."

"Yeah, man. The weather dude said the storm blew south and is dumping much more snow on us than expected."

"How much?"

"Ten to twelve inches here. Six to eight where you are."

"Overnight?"

"Yeah."

"Fuck," I mumbled.

"What are you gonna do? Do you want me to call your dad?" he asked. I cringed at how his question sounded and hoped Aspen didn't hear him.

"Nah. I'll be fine. I'm actually sitting in the cab of the truck in the lane next to me."

"You sure? Because I was kind of hoping Shaker could fly in and drop a rope down to you."

"Yeah, I'm sure," I laughed. "But you can let my boss know I'm not going to make it to work in the morning."

He laughed. "Will do. Stay safe, brother."

"Did you say morning?" Aspen asked as soon as the phone left my ear.

I nodded solemnly. "Yeah. That was my roommate. He was watching the news, and they said motorists would likely be stranded until morning. He also told me we're getting several inches more snow than originally expected."

She slumped back in her seat, and a look of worry washed over her face.

"You okay?"

"I'm fine," she said distractedly. "I'm just trying to figure out how I'm going to drive this monster truck the rest of the way home through snow and ice. Because I'm going to be really honest here; I wasn't doing such a great job when the roads were clear."

I completely understood where she was coming from. I was an experienced rider, but I'd never ridden through snow and ice, and I didn't want to learn in snow almost a foot deep. However, I had no problem driving a vehicle while it was snowing.

"How much room do you have back there?" I asked and gestured to the truck behind us with my thumb.

"I don't know," she said with a hint of confusion. "A lot. Why?"

"Will my bike fit?"

She tilted her head to the side and studied me for a few moments while she thought about my question.

"It will if you're offering to drive when traffic starts moving again."

"I am," I said and extended my hand. "Deal?"

"Deal," she said and placed her hand in mine once again.

And once again, I ignored how much I liked the feel of her soft hand in mine.

Surprisingly, loading my bike into the back of her moving truck was easier than expected. The truck was equipped with a ramp, and there was plenty of room as almost half the truck was empty.

While I secured my bike, she rummaged around through some of her packed belongings. When we returned to the warmth of the cab, she spread out a small blanket between us and dumped out the contents of the bag she was holding. "Want something to eat or drink?"

I looked down at the pile of snacks and bottles of flavored water and smiled. "I'm starving."

"Help yourself."

So I did. I was well into my second bag of chips when I realized I was the only one enjoying snack time.

"You're not hungry?" I asked.

"No, I already ate," she said.

And then her stomach growled.

She slapped a hand over her abdomen and shook her head. "Okay, fine. I'm hungry. But if I eat, I'll have to drink. And if I drink, I'll have to pee. And there's nowhere to really do that."

"Go in the back of the truck. You should have some kind of bucket or container back there," I suggested.

She scrunched her nose. "I guess I could do that if I had to."

When I loaded my bike in the back of her truck, I grabbed my iPad from my saddle bag and brought it into the cab with me. I held it up for her to see. "Want to watch a movie?"

"Sure, as long as it isn't a horror movie."

"No horror. Noted," I said and scrolled through the options. "How about this one? I think there are five total, so we could essentially have a movie marathon while we wait this out."

She smiled. "Works for me."

"Have you seen any of these movies before?"

"No. I wanted to but never got around to it. You?"

"Nope. They're new to me too."

After the first movie, she went to the back of the truck to get some more food while I stepped out to take a piss. Several inches of snow had accumulated on the ground, and it was still steadily coming down.

She climbed back into the truck carrying a grocery bag of items. "Do you want a peanut butter and jelly sandwich?"

"I'd love one."

"It's actually jam, not jelly," she pointed out.

"That's fine. I'm not picky."

"I kind of am. At least about this. I think jelly is gross, but jam's cool."

I laughed. "I'm not sure I knew there was a difference."

"There definitely is," she said seriously.

When I took a bite of the best peanut butter and jelly sandwich I'd ever had, I thought she might be right about the jam.

We were well into the second movie when her head started to droop. She raised it quickly, then yawned.

"I hope you're not trying to stay awake on my account."

"Are we allowed to go to sleep?" she asked.

"Why wouldn't we be?"

"Because we're in the middle of the highway. How will we know when traffic starts moving again?"

"If we're not already awake, one of us will hear engines cranking and horns honking."

"I don't know if I'll be able to sleep."

Before I could ask why, my phone rang. I looked at the screen and cringed. Both of my mothers were expecting me to call or text when I got home.

"Hey, Mom. I know I haven't called, but in my defense, I'm not home yet," I said without giving her a chance to speak.

"Please tell me you aren't one of the ones stuck in that mess on the highway," she said, her voice full of worry.

"Sorry, Mom, but before you freak out, I'm inside the cab of a truck. I'm warm and dry."

"Oh, thank goodness," she sighed and then inhaled sharply. "Are you safe? Does he look like a serial killer? Can he hear me?"

I shook my head and laughed while I put my phone on speaker. "It doesn't matter if she can hear you or not. She's gonna know what you asked when I answer. Yes, I'm safe. No, she doesn't look like a serial killer, and I'm not sure. Aspen, can you hear my overprotective mother?"

Aspen giggled. "Yes, ma'am, I can hear you."

My mother's tone changed immediately. "Oh, sweetheart, my name's Kathleen. Now, I know my son may look a little rough with his leather clothes and motorcycle, but I assure you, you have nothing to worry about. He's a good boy."

"I look rough?" I teased. "That hurts a little, Mom."

"Hush. Now, can she still hear me?"

"She can."

"Thank you for getting my baby out of the cold. I had a feeling he was out there when he hadn't called."

"You're welcome. There was no way I could let him sit out there and freeze. And he's been great company."

"That's my boy," she said proudly.

"All right, Mom," I said, ready to wrap things up.

"I'm glad you're safe and warm. Keep me updated and call Annabelle," she said.

"I will. Love you."

"Love you, too," she said and ended the call.

"Excuse me while I make this other phone call before I forget," I said and dialed my other mother.

She picked up on the first ring.

"Coal! Oh, thank goodness! I was just about to call you. Are you home?"

"Not yet," I said and explained my current situation to her.

"Hold on a sec. Let me see if there's anything your dad can do."

There wasn't, and I heard him say as much a few moments later. "Doll face, if he can't get out, I can't get to him. He's safe and warm. He'll be fine."

"I don't like any of this. How are you going to ride through the snow and ice when traffic starts moving again?"

I quickly explained the deal I'd made with Aspen, and her response was very similar to the one I'd previously received. "Is she scared of you?"

I laughed. "You and Mom are giving me a complex."

"Well, honey, you're a biker. A big one at that. You might be one of my babies, but apparently, I produce scary babies."

"Ember's not—," I started and laughed. "Wait. Yes, she is."

Mom laughed too. "See what I mean?"

"I sure do. All right, Mom, I'm going to go. I'll make sure to keep you updated."

"Thanks, son. I love you."

"Love you, too," I said and ended the call.

"Sorry about that."

"No need to apologize," she said with a curious look

on her face. And I had a feeling I knew exactly why. "Go ahead and ask."

"You have two mothers?" she blurted immediately.

Even though I was expecting the question, I wasn't sure how to answer it. I'd never had to explain it to anyone because everyone I was around already knew the story.

"Yes, I do. Without going into too much detail, I was adopted at birth and reconnected with my biological parents when I was nineteen. Kathleen is my adoptive mother, and Annabelle is my biological mother."

"Seems like they both really care about you."

Of course they did. They were my mothers. Which made me wonder if maybe her mother didn't care about her. But I wasn't going to ask. Instead, I told her they did and changed the subject.

* * *

I DON'T KNOW WHEN I FELL ASLEEP, BUT THE SUDDEN roar of engines woke me.

I looked down to see Aspen asleep in my lap where my iPad had once been. Apparently, we'd fallen asleep during one of the movies and had sort of folded in on each other. I wasn't complaining. I was just glad my dick wasn't poking her in the forehead.

"Aspen," I said softly while gently shaking her shoulder.

"What?" she gasped and immediately sat up, banging her head into my chin as she did. "Ow, fuck. Shit. Are you okay?"

I groaned and rubbed my chin. "I don't know. Are

all my teeth still there?" I asked and flashed her a toothy grin.

"I think so," she nodded while rubbing the back of her head. "I'm so sorry."

"It's fine," I said and reached out to caress the back of her head. "Are you okay?"

She froze, with her eyes locked on mine, and slowly nodded. "Yeah, I think so."

I gestured toward the steering wheel. "Do you still want me to drive? I think things are about to get moving."

"Yes, I do!" she exclaimed and climbed over me to the passenger's seat while I moved over behind the wheel.

It took a while for us to get moving, and even then, it was stop-and-go for miles.

I glanced at the gas gauge and noticed we had less than a quarter of a tank. "I'm going to take the next exit so we can get gas."

What I thought would be a quick trip turned out to be anything but. Traffic was moving at a snail's pace as soon as we got off the exit.

"Looks like everyone else had the same idea you did," she observed.

"This is ridiculous," I said as we inched down the road. The gas station was still miles away, and at the rate we were going, it would take us all day to get there.

And then it started snowing again.

"I didn't think we were supposed to get more snow," she said when she noticed the flurries landing on the windshield.

"We weren't," I said, but the grey clouds covering the sky said otherwise.

"No offense, but I don't think I can stand being trapped in this capsule of fun for another fourteen hours."

"I saw a hotel when we got off the highway."

She straightened in her seat. "What are you saying?"

"We could go back and get a room. I wouldn't mind a warm shower and a long nap while we wait this out," I suggested, hoping she would be agreeable.

She exhaled in relief. "That sounds wonderful."

I turned around in the next parking lot we came to and drove the few miles back to the hotel.

3

ASPEN

I really didn't have the extra funds to spend on a hotel room, but I was exhausted and wanted to be out of that truck more than I'd wanted anything in a long time.

Coal parked the truck and turned to me. "I'd like to pay for your room."

"Oh, no, I couldn't—"

"You burned through a lot of gas keeping me warm last night. It's the least I can do."

I hadn't even considered the gas consumption, but I would have burned through the same amount of gas with or without him. However, I really didn't have the extra money to spend on a hotel room, particularly since I was currently unemployed. And I didn't want to tell him any of that.

"I'd feel bad taking up two rooms when there's only two of us. Maybe we could share one?" I suggested.

He grinned. "Works for me. I need to grab a change of clothes from my bike. Do you need anything from the back before we go inside?"

I nodded. "Yes, I need clothes too, and I'll grab some more snacks."

After gathering our belongings, we made our way into the hotel and reserved a room. The hotel itself wasn't anything fancy, just your average three-star hotel along the side of a highway. But after spending fourteen hours in a moving truck at a standstill on the snow-covered highway, it felt like the lap of luxury.

"Do you want to shower first?" he asked.

"No, you go ahead. I couldn't find my toothbrush. I'm going to go down to the gift shop to see if they have one."

I actually did know where my toothbrush was, but I really needed to poop and didn't want to do that with him in close proximity, so I made up an excuse to go find a bathroom somewhere else.

After taking care of business, I stopped by the gift shop and bought a toothbrush to corroborate my story. Then, I made a phone call I should have made the night before.

“Hey, Aspen. I was starting to get worried about you. Did you make it to Devil Springs okay?”

“Actually, no, I didn't. It started snowing, and I got stuck in that mess on the highway. I'm going to spend the night at a hotel and try again in the morning.”

“Okay,” he said, sounding distracted. “Thanks for calling. Let me know when you finally get there.”

“Will do,” I promised and headed back to my room.

I opened the door to the hotel room and took a few steps inside before I looked up and came to a complete stop. Coal was standing a few feet away with clothes in one hand and a towel wrapped around his waist. When he looked at me, his bright blue eyes widened as water dripped from his dark blonde hair.

"Sorry," he said sheepishly. "I hate getting dressed in a steamy bathroom, and you weren't in here when I checked two seconds ago."

I should have stepped to the side and let him continue to the bathroom, but I couldn't take my eyes off his abdomen. Yes, he had muscles and ripples for days. Even the coveted V that makes so many women drool, myself included. But that's not what had me staring at him like I had absolutely no manners.

Before I could stop myself, I closed the gap between us and reached out to trace one of his scars with the tip of my finger. "What happened?"

We stood in silence for what felt like an eternity, with my finger still gently resting against his scarred skin. Enough time for me to realize I had asked a question I had no business asking.

"I'm sorry," I said and took a step back. "You don't have to answer. That was incredibly rude of me to ask."

He cleared his throat and wrapped his hand around mine. "It's fine. I was shot three times. These spots are where the bullets went in," he said and moved my finger to each of the rounded scars. Two were close together near the middle of his stomach while one was off to the side by itself. "And the straight lines are from where the surgeon went in to get them."

"Can I ask what happened?" I asked while tucking my hands into my pockets to keep them from touching anything else they shouldn't.

"You can," he grinned, "but I can't tell you."

I nodded, reluctantly accepting his answer, but I wasn't sure if he didn't want to talk about it because it was a traumatic event or if he wasn't telling me for a different, possibly darker, reason.

"But you're okay now?" I asked, trying to hide how awkward I felt.

"Yep," he said. "All good."

"Let me grab my clothes, and I'll get out of your way so you can get dressed," I said and made a mad dash for the bathroom.

Once in the shower, I took my time and emerged feeling much more refreshed than I thought possible.

Coal was talking to someone on the phone but ended the call shortly after he noticed me.

"How was your shower?" he asked.

"Great. I feel like a new woman," I joked.

"Are you hungry? I was thinking about ordering room service."

"That sounds perfect. I'm starving." The sandwiches we'd had the night before were long gone, and neither one of us had anything for breakfast.

While we were waiting for our food to be delivered, I called the place where I'd rented the moving truck and explained my situation. Thankfully, the woman on the phone was very understanding and told me I could keep the truck until Thursday at no additional charge. I thanked her profusely and promised to leave them a great review online.

"What made you decide to move to Devil Springs?" Coal asked shortly after our food arrived.

"I lived in Devil Springs before I moved to Cherryfield when I was eighteen. It just wasn't the place for me, so I decided to move back when the lease on my apartment was up."

"Do you have family in town?"

"Sort of. Technically, my stepfather lives there, but he works out of town and is rarely home."

I could tell he was about to ask another question, likely about my mother, and I did not want to discuss her whatsoever, so I quickly shifted the focus to him. "What about you? Are you from Devil Springs?"

He swallowed the bite of food in his mouth before answering. "No, I grew up in Croftridge and moved to Devil Springs when I was nineteen."

"May I ask why?"

"Have you heard of the Blackwings MC?"

I snorted. "I don't think it's possible to live in Devil Springs for any length of time and not know who they are."

He chuckled. "Yeah, I suppose you're right about that. I'm a member of the club. I joined the Croftridge chapter and transferred to the Devil Springs chapter a year later."

I wanted to ask why. The question was on the tip of my tongue, but I didn't want to be too invasive, just like I didn't want him to be with me.

I glanced out the window at the still-falling snow. "How long do you think the snow will last?"

He shrugged. "I'd say several days at least."

"I have to have the truck back by Thursday. Do you think the roads will be clear by then?"

"They should be, but if you're worried about it, I can drive the truck back for you."

"Oh, no, I can't ask you to do that."

"You didn't ask. I offered."

"Are you sure? It'll take most of the day to get there and back."

"I'm sure. I'm off on Thursday and don't have any other plans."

"If you really don't mind, I'd greatly appreciate it," I admitted.

"Trust me; it won't be a hardship. Especially with such great company," he winked, causing my stomach to do a little flip.

"Thanks. You're not so bad yourself."

Even though he was basically a complete stranger, I felt comfortable with him. He was easy to talk to and seemed like a nice guy. He was also insanely attractive, but I was doing my best to ignore that.

"Do you want to finish the movie marathon we started last night?" Coal asked after we finished eating.

"Sure, but I can't promise to stay awake. I haven't gotten much sleep the last few nights, and I think it's starting to catch up with me."

"I know what you mean. After last night, I could use a good night's sleep myself," he said.

I struggled to stay awake during the first two movies, knowing if I fell asleep too early, I'd wake up in the middle of the night and not be able to go back to sleep. I dozed off somewhere during the third movie, but it wasn't the restful sleep I'd hoped for.

"You're the reason I went to prison, and it's time you paid for it," my mother sneered and slapped me across the face.

I stood frozen in place, unable to move, no matter how hard I tried.

"I never should've given birth to you. You were always such a pain in my ass. I can't wait to finally be rid of you. I should've done this years ago." She wrapped her hands around my throat and squeezed.

I couldn't scream. I couldn't breathe. I couldn't do anything but stand there as she choked the life out of me with a look of evil glee on her face.

"Aspen. Wake up. You're having a nightmare," a familiar voice said in the distance, but I was still frozen, trapped between my dreams and reality.

Then, I felt strong arms wrap around me and pull me against a solid chest. "You're okay. It was just a dream," Coal soothed.

I turned in his arms and snuggled against his chest, relishing in the comfort and security I so desperately needed. I was far too upset to even think about being embarrassed.

When I woke the next morning, Coal was already awake and having a cup of coffee. "Morning," I said and sat up in bed.

"Good morning," he replied and studied me. "You okay?"

I felt my cheeks heat. I was hoping he wouldn't mention it, but I had no such luck. "Uh, yeah, I'm good. Sorry about all that. I don't usually have bad dreams."

He shrugged like it was no big deal. "It happens."

"So, what's the plan for today?"

"I was thinking we could leave after breakfast. According to the news, the secondary roads are still in rough shape, but the highway is mostly clear. It will probably take longer than usual, but we should be able to get home today."

4

COAL

Four hours later, we finally arrived in Devil Springs. Game was right. It really did look like a snow-covered ghost town. Very few businesses were open, and virtually no one was out and about.

Once we hit the main part of town, Aspen started giving me turn-by-turn directions to her house. As we got closer, I realized I was familiar with the area. Very familiar. When she pointed to her house, I pulled into her driveway and grinned. "This is where you live?"

"Yes. Why?"

I pointed to the house directly behind hers. "Because that's my house. Looks like we're neighbors."

She smiled. "I guess I don't need to worry about you making it home okay since you don't have far to go."

"You were worried about me?" I teased.

"Maybe a little."

Her words made my heart flutter. I liked that she cared.

While I unloaded my bike, she picked up a box and

carried it inside, returning almost immediately with a look of concern on her face.

"Something wrong?"

"The power's out."

"Shit. If yours is out, I'm sure mine is too." I glanced around and didn't see any houses with lights on in the vicinity.

"I wonder how long it will be before it's back on."

"I don't know, but you can't stay here without power. It's too cold. You can come to the clubhouse with me."

"Say what now?"

"The MC clubhouse. We have generators, so we never lose power. You can stay there with me until our power's restored."

She seemed hesitant, so I continued. "It'll probably only be for one night. But if you don't come with me, I'm going to stay here and freeze with you."

She narrowed her eyes. "Oh, that's dirty."

"I'm willing to play dirty when I need to."

She exhaled slowly. "If you're sure it's okay."

"It's more than okay," I assured her. "Grab what you want to take with you. I'll go home and get my truck and pick you up in a few minutes."

When she nodded in agreement, I quickly left before she had a chance to change her mind.

She must have been watching for me because she came out the front door carrying a backpack as soon as I pulled up.

"I've never been to a biker clubhouse before. Is there anything I need to know?"

I laughed. "We're regular, everyday people. You'll be fine," I said, and then another thought occurred to me.

"The clubhouse will likely be packed with the members and their families since it seems like the majority of Devil Springs is without power. And they're probably going to assume you're my girlfriend, even if we say otherwise."

"Really? Why?"

"Because there's only a few of us left that haven't gotten married or claimed an Old Lady, and according to some, 'it's my turn.' So, when I show up with a pretty girl on my arm, they're going to be all over it."

"Wow, no pressure or anything."

"Right? At least Layla hasn't created a profile for me on one of those dating apps yet. Well, I don't think she has."

Aspen laughed. "I'm sorry, but that's hilarious. Has she done that before?"

"Yes, but I don't think she did it behind his back. I'm pretty sure he knew about it."

"I've always been too scared to use dating apps. It'd be my luck to end up matching with a psycho serial killer or something."

It was the perfect segue to ask if she was seeing anyone. I didn't think she was since she hadn't mentioned a boyfriend. She actually hadn't mentioned anyone other than her stepfather. But I didn't want to scare her off or make her feel obligated in any kind of way since she was relying on me to some degree.

As I suspected, the parking lot at the clubhouse was overflowing with cars.

"Do you want to go in the front and meet everyone now or try to sneak in the back way?"

"Might as well meet everyone now and get it over with."

"It might be overwhelming, but I promise, everyone in that building is a good person."

We walked to the front doors, and I stepped inside first so she wouldn't have to. The room quieted down, and all eyes turned to us.

"Hey, everyone. This is Aspen. She's my new neighbor, and she's going to be staying with us while her power's out."

Brinkley appeared from the crowd and ran toward us. "You look like Merida!"

"Thank you. She's my favorite princess. What's your name?" Aspen asked with a smile.

"My name's Brinkley Moore, and my mommy's name is Mackenzie Moore, and Mr. Bear is her fancy."

"Fiancé," I whispered.

"And Coal is my babysitter."

I reached down and scooped Brinkley into my arms, tickling her sides as I did.

"Stop! Stop!" she squealed through her laughter. "I'm gonna tell my big brother on you."

I laughed and handed her off to Batta, who'd made his way over to us. "You taught her to say that, didn't you?"

He shrugged. "Maybe."

"Can we go play in the snow?" Brinkley asked.

"You just came back inside. How about a cookie instead?"

"Yes, please."

"Save some for me!" Bronze shouted.

"Might as well start with him. That's Bronze. He's the VP and also my cousin. The baby in his arms is his daughter, Blue, and the woman beside him is his fiancée,

Sloane," I said and continued around the room until everyone had been introduced.

Aspen smiled and nodded, but she looked completely overwhelmed by the time I was finished.

"It's okay. No one expects you to remember everyone's name," Layla said.

"Oh good, because I was a little worried about that," she admitted.

"No need to worry. We're a friendly bunch. Would you two like something to eat or drink?" Layla offered.

"Yes, but let me show her to her room first."

"About that. We're full. So your room is her room."

I wasn't sure how Aspen felt about it, but I was quite happy about having to share my room with her.

"Right this way," I said and took her hand in mine to pull her along with me. I wasn't even aware I'd done it until we were standing in my room, and I had to force myself to let go.

"I'm sorry about the room situation. I didn't realize the clubhouse would be full, but you can take the bed, and I'll sleep on the floor."

"Absolutely not. You're the one doing me a favor. If anyone's sleeping on the floor, it's me," she insisted.

"You're not sleeping on the floor."

"We've already slept beside each other for the last two nights. I don't think one more is going to be an issue."

"As long as you're comfortable with it."

"I'll be fine," she assured me.

While she might be fine, I wasn't entirely sure I would be. After climbing in bed with her and holding her through her nightmares, I'd woken up with her ass nestled against me and a raging hard-on I could do nothing about.

"Are you hungry?"

"I could eat."

"I'm not sure what they have, but the food's always good," I told her as we walked to the common room.

They had a table set up in a corner of the room with everything needed for tacos.

"Oh, this is perfect," Aspen said happily. "I love tacos." She loaded her plate with three and turned to me. "Where should we sit?"

I pointed to an empty table in the opposite corner of the room. "Over there, so maybe we can eat in peace."

"Do you want a beer or something else to drink?" I asked once she was seated.

"Yeah, I'll take a beer."

"Be right back."

I returned just as Game was sitting down at the table with Aspen. "I hear you're our new neighbor."

She nodded. "Yep. And your name's Game, right?"

"Yes. Well, my real name is Grant. My road name is Game. I'll answer to either," he said with a smile.

"Have you heard when the power's supposed to be back on?" I asked.

"The outage line says by eleven o'clock Thursday night."

"What?" Aspen gasped. "That's two days from now."

Game nodded. "The storm did a lot of damage. They've had to bring in other companies from out of town to help with the repairs. Otherwise, it'd take a lot longer."

"I can't wait that long. I have to return the moving

truck by Thursday."

"You still can. We can go over and unload everything tomorrow during the day and come back here to spend the night before we take the truck back Thursday morning."

"Let me know what time tomorrow. Drew and I will tag along to help," Game offered.

"Oh, no, you guys don't have to do that," Aspen protested.

"I know, but it's not like we have anything else to do. Everything's closed, and I'm not a sit around and do nothing kind of guy," Game said.

"Thank you. I really could use the help. I was lucky I didn't get seriously injured when I loaded the truck by myself. And to be honest, I wasn't looking forward to unloading it on my own."

"You loaded it by yourself?" I asked in disbelief. "How in the hell did you manage to get your mattress in there without help?"

"With a lot of blood, sweat, and cuss words, but it was the sofa that almost killed me."

"You won't have to worry about that tomorrow. Between the four of us, it shouldn't take long to empty the truck."

We stayed in the common room and had a few more beers with Game before returning to my room.

"Is it okay if I take a shower?" she asked.

"Of course. Clean towels are under the sink. Help yourself to whatever you need."

"Thanks. I shouldn't be long."

"Take your time," I insisted. She didn't need to rush on my account.

She returned a short time later smelling like a

cupcake and looking even better. She was wearing a snug tank top that showcased her full breasts and a tight pair of leggings that clung to her shapely ass. We hadn't even gotten into bed together, and I was already dying a slow death.

"All finished," she announced and walked around to the far side of the bed. "Is it okay if I sleep on this side?"

"You can sleep on whichever side you want."

"Which side would you sleep on if I wasn't here?"

"This one," I said and pointed to the side closest to the bathroom. "But it really doesn't matter to me." And it didn't, although I thought it was sweet of her to ask. From what I'd seen so far, she seemed to be naturally considerate of other people. Something I found quite endearing.

She further proved my observation to be true when she said, "Let me know when you're finished. I'll step out of the room so you don't have to get dressed in the bathroom."

There was no way in hell I was going to let that happen. Not with what she was wearing.

"I appreciate it, but I'll be fine," I said and disappeared into the bathroom.

I didn't linger in the shower, even though I desperately wanted to rub one out before I had to get into bed with her. I wish I could say I didn't because it somehow seemed disrespectful, but the one and only reason I kept my hand off of my dick was because I didn't want to take the risk of her hearing me. The clubhouse walls were thin, and based on the things I'd heard over the years, not everyone knew it. Or maybe they did and just didn't care.

5

ASPEN

I was a bit nervous about going to sleep. Not because I was in bed with an attractive man who was also kind and caring, though that should have been reason enough. No, I was worried about having another nightmare. The dream was so intense and vivid, unlike any dream I'd had before. It felt real, and it was terrifying. I had no interest in experiencing anything like it ever again.

"Something on your mind?" Coal asked when I changed positions for the umpteenth time.

I sighed. I didn't want to tell him everything, but I thought getting some of it off my chest might help. "I don't want to have another nightmare," I confessed and hated how weak I sounded.

He reached for me and pulled me to him, slipping an arm around me and cradling my head against his bare chest. "Tell me what it was about."

"Someone was in my house, and they were trying to kill me. They were choking me, and I couldn't do anything to stop them."

"Do you know who it was?"

I should've expected that question, but I didn't, and hesitated to answer, which I'm sure he noticed.

"It was a woman."

"Hmm." He was silent for a few moments while he thought. "Maybe you're subconsciously nervous about moving back to Devil Springs, and it's presenting itself in your dreams."

"Yeah, I guess I am in a way. I mean, I've lived here before, but it was years ago. And this time, I'll be living alone instead of with my stepdad."

"And I'll be right behind you if you need anything."

"I still can't believe you live in the house behind me. What a crazy coincidence," I said, trying to shift to a lighter topic.

"Maybe," he said quietly. "Or maybe it was meant to be." At least, that's what I thought he said. And the more I thought about it, it's what I hoped he said.

* * *

The power was still out when we arrived at my house to unload the moving truck. It was almost as cold inside as it was outside. I didn't think moving was fun on a good day, but moving while freezing my ass off was horrible. I was more than ready to go back to the warm clubhouse by the time we were finished.

"Are you sure you don't want us to put some of your furniture back together?" Game asked.

I pointed to my chattering teeth. "If it wasn't so cold, I'd say yes, but I'm freezing."

The disappointment on Game's face was evident.

"If you really want to, you're welcome to stay and put stuff together," I offered. "But I'm leaving."

He grinned. "Do you have a spare key so I can lock up when I leave?"

"Let me check," I said and rummaged through the junk drawer in the kitchen where we used to keep a spare key. Luckily, it was still there.

"Thank you for all of your help today," I said and handed him the key.

"Anytime. I don't like snow, and I've been bored out of my mind being stuck inside. I'm happy to have something to do."

"I guess this works out well for the both of us."

"You ready to go?" Coal asked.

"Definitely," I said and followed him to his truck. I climbed inside and smiled when I noticed he'd turned my seat warmer on for me.

"I need to stop by my house and grab some clothes. Do you want to come in?"

"Maybe another time. I'll stay here where it's nice and warm."

"I'll be right back."

While he was inside, his phone rang, and the name Ember appeared on his truck's screen. Feelings of jealousy shot through me at seeing a woman's name. Feelings I had no right to have. Coal and I were friends, nothing more. Regardless, I still didn't like it.

His phone stopped ringing and dinged with a text message, which I shamelessly read since a preview popped up on his lock screen.

Ember: Haven't heard from you in a few days. Call me. Love you.

I stared at the phone and scrunched my nose in disgust. Who the hell was Ember? Was she his girlfriend that he'd been avoiding for the last few days because he'd been with me? More importantly, how was I going to find out without sounding like the jealous woman I clearly was?

I was still trying to figure that out when Coal returned with a duffel bag in tow. He climbed into the truck, glanced at his phone, looked at me, and laughed.

"What?" I asked, trying not to sound defensive and failing miserably.

"Ember's my twin sister," he explained.

I tried to play dumb. "What are you talking about?"

He didn't buy my act. "The girl that just called and text. Ember. She's my twin sister."

I still refused to acknowledge what he was implying. Instead, I tried to redirect. "You have a twin sister?"

"I do," he confirmed. "She lives in Croftridge with her husband and their daughter."

"Do you have any other siblings?"

He nodded. "I have a half brother named Nathan, who's a year younger than me. And I have a younger brother and sister who are also twins. They're two years old."

"Wow, sounds like twins run in your family."

"I guess so. What about you? Do you have any siblings?"

"Nope, it's just me," I said. I honestly didn't know if I had any brothers or sisters, and I wasn't interested in finding out. But that wasn't something easy to explain, so once again I changed the subject before he could ask me anything else about my family.

"What time should we leave tomorrow?"

"I was thinking we could head out around ten or so. Does that work for you?"

"You're the one driving, so it's really whatever works for you."

* * *

Once again, I spent the night wrapped in Coal's arms and woke nightmare free. Neither of us said a word about how we were sleeping, and I wasn't sure if that made things more or less awkward. It did leave me with numerous questions.

Was he just being kind, or was there more to it?

Did I want there to be more to it?

Yes. Yes, I did, I finally admitted to myself. But I didn't want to risk ruining our new friendship to find out.

So, I kept my feelings to myself and suffered in silence. Not that being around Coal could be considered any kind of suffering. Quite the opposite, actually.

The drive to Cherryfield was uneventful, for which I was grateful. Part of me expected for us to get caught in another storm or be stuck in traffic because of a wreck. But that wasn't the case. We dropped the truck off, picked up my car, and stopped for lunch before we headed back.

He offered to drive my car back to Devil Springs, and I happily accepted. I preferred to be a passenger when I had the option, especially on long trips. Which worked out great for us because he preferred to drive.

Game called while we were on our way home to let us know the power had been restored to our neighborhood. While I was happy to have power, I found myself disappointed that I wouldn't get to spend another night with Coal. And the thought of spending the night alone in the house I once shared with my mother was even more daunting.

"You're awfully quiet over there," Coal observed.

"Sorry, I was just thinking about all of the things I need to do now that my impromptu vacation is over."

"Like what?"

"The usual stuff that goes along with moving—unpacking, getting settled, grocery shopping, changing my address," I explained.

Before I was ready, we were back at my house. I really didn't want him to go but couldn't think of a reason to ask him to stay. He gave me his phone number and asked for mine, and told me to call him if I needed help with anything. Then, he was gone.

I couldn't explain it, but I felt more alone in that moment than I had in a long time, if ever.

Since there wasn't much I could do about it, I went inside and started unpacking, hoping that would keep me somewhat occupied.

I'd been at it for a few hours and had made quite a bit of progress when my stomach growled.

"Shit," I grumbled, knowing there was nothing to eat in the house. I really didn't feel like going to the grocery store, so I ordered a pizza for delivery and promised myself I'd go to the store the next day.

I thought about texting Coal to see if he wanted to come over for pizza, but decided against it.

When the pizza arrived, I noticed a package on the front porch. I brought it inside with the food and looked at the label. It had my address on it, but it was for someone named S.M. Gal. There was no return address or anything else on the package to indicate where it was from.

"Guess I'll take it to the post office tomorrow while I'm out," I said to myself and reached for a slice of pizza.

6

COAL

I felt like a stalker. My bedroom was on the back side of the house, and I couldn't stop looking at Aspen's house from my bedroom window.

It was close to midnight, and she still had most of the lights on. I wondered if it was because she was busy unpacking or if she was having trouble sleeping. And I couldn't ask her without sounding like the total creeper I was.

"You've got it bad, brother," Game said from behind me.

I turned and glared. "Don't you know how to knock?"

"I did knock. Twice."

"What if I was doing something you didn't need to see?"

"Then you would've been in the bathroom," he said knowingly.

"Fuck off," I grumbled and held up my middle finger for good measure.

He laughed and raised his hands up in mock

surrender. "I just wanted to make sure you knew the gym will be open tomorrow. I wasn't sure if anyone told you."

"No, no one did, but I assumed it would be when I saw the power on when I drove by earlier today."

"All right. Well, don't stay up too late."

I picked up my shoe and chucked it at him, but he closed the door before it hit him.

I didn't care that he was teasing me about Aspen. What bothered me was that he noticed to begin with. Had I been that obvious?

As I turned back to my window, I realized maybe I had. And then I thought, why did it matter?

* * *

When my alarm went off the next morning, I had to drag myself out of bed. Aspen stayed up until well after one o'clock in the morning, which meant I had too. Then, I tossed and turned all night, waking up at least once every hour. Hopefully, it would be a slow day, and I'd have a chance to catch a nap in my office.

Unfortunately, I had no such luck. The gym was packed almost from the moment we opened the doors. One employee called in sick, and then Bronze had to leave early to take Blue to the doctor. Which meant I had to fill in for him as a sparring partner for one of the fighters he was training for Lorcan.

I usually didn't mind sparring with the fighters. It was a great workout and helped me keep my skills finely tuned. But I was tired from the lack of sleep, and Bronze was working with my least favorite of the fighters. I couldn't say why, but there was something about the guy I didn't like.

So, when he landed a kick to my ribs much harder than anyone should have in a practice setting, I didn't hesitate to put him in his place.

"What the fuck?" he screamed. "You broke my fucking nose!"

"And you damn near broke my ribs! This is practice. You pull your punches and kicks. I won't tell you again."

"Shane, go get cleaned up and get out of here. You're done for the day," Savior said and stepped into the ring.

"This is bullshit!" Shane yelled and stormed off like an angry child.

"Let's have a look," Savior said and carefully raised my shirt. "Damn. It might be broken."

"It better not be."

"I'll get some ice and meet you upstairs."

He found me resting awkwardly on the couch in my office. I wasn't comfortable by any means, but it was the only position I could manage that didn't make my ribs hurt worse.

I groaned in pain when he placed the bag of ice on my side.

"I'm going to have a word with Bronze about him. He's hurt two other fighters since he's been here, and he consistently has a bad attitude."

"Maybe he got the adjustment he needed today."

"Dude, you should've seen it from where I was standing. His feet came off the ground, and he went flying when you hit him."

"You'll have to save the video for me so I can watch it when it doesn't hurt to laugh."

"Why don't you go ahead and go home for the day? Game and I can handle things until Bronze gets back," he suggested.

"Yeah, I think I will. My bed will be much more comfortable than this couch."

I was right. My bed was better, but getting to it was hell. I felt every bump and bounce on the way home. Not to mention, some woman on a cell phone pulled out in front of me, and I had to slam on my brakes to keep from plowing into her.

Once I made it home, I crawled into bed, happy I was at least getting to take the nap I'd been hoping for all day. I was almost asleep when my phone dinged with a text.

"Mother fucker," I growled in frustration and damn near ripped the cord out of the wall when I snatched my phone from my nightstand. But my mood suddenly changed when I saw who it was from.

Aspen: I was wondering if I could make dinner for you tonight to thank you for all of your help this week.

Coal: I'd like that. What time?

Aspen: Can you be here around seven?

Coal: Yes. Can I bring anything?

Aspen: Just your appetite.

Coal: See you at seven.

I didn't care how much pain I was in. I was not going to miss a chance to have dinner with Aspen. Just the thought of seeing her made me feel a little bit better.

* * *

I HOPED I WOULD BE ABLE TO HIDE MY INJURY FROM HER, but she noticed the awkward way I was standing the moment she opened the door.

"Are you okay? What happened?" she asked and reached for my arm to help me inside.

"I got kicked in the ribs at work today."

"What? How?"

Suddenly, I realized she didn't know what I did for a living.

"I work at the gym downtown on Jefferson Street. I was sparring with one of the fighters who trains with us and took a hard kick to the ribs." I refrained from telling her that I thought he did it on purpose, or that I broke his nose in return.

"You should've told me. We could've done dinner another night."

I shrugged. "Even though I'm hurt, I still need to eat."

She shook her head at my response and led me to her couch. "Come sit down and make yourself comfortable. Dinner's almost ready."

"It smells delicious."

"It's baked ziti and garlic bread. And tiramisu for dessert. I hope you like it."

"I'm sure I will."

And I did. Which I told her as soon as I took my first

bite. I pointed at my plate with my fork and swallowed. "This is really good."

"Thanks," she beamed. "I enjoy cooking but don't get the chance to do it as often as I'd like."

"Why's that?"

"It's hard to cook a nice meal for just one person without wasting a lot of food," she explained.

"We should work something out where Game and I buy the food and you do the cooking," I suggested, only half joking.

"I like that idea."

"Really? Maybe we could give it a try. Not every day, but maybe once or twice a week."

"Speaking of Game, do you want to invite him to join us?"

"I would, but he's still at work," I said, knowing damn well I wouldn't have asked him to join us if he wasn't.

"Oh, well, I'll send a plate for him home with you."

"Thanks. I know he'll appreciate it. If we don't eat at the clubhouse, we usually have takeout. Home-cooked meals like this are a rare treat."

"Sounds like we really should work out a dinner plan."

I was all for it if it meant I was guaranteed to see her once or twice a week.

I glanced around and noticed the pile of empty boxes by the back door. "Looks like you got a lot done today."

"I did," she said proudly. "I'm almost finished unpacking. I also took care of a few errands, and I found a job."

"That's great. Where are you going to be working?"

"At a bookstore in town. I start Monday," she said excitedly.

"It wouldn't happen to be Books, Books, and Books, would it?"

"Yes. Are you familiar with it?"

I grinned. "The gym I work at is next door to the bookstore."

"Are you kidding?"

I shook my head. "Not at all. Maybe we can take a lunch break together sometime."

"I'd like that," she smiled.

I was a little curious as to how she got hired at the bookstore. I thought it was a front for other operations, and they only hired people who were specially trained for said operations.

After dinner, I offered to help her clean up, but she refused to let me. "I'll take care of this. You need to go home and rest. It's obvious you're in pain."

She was right, and I hated Shane a little bit more for ruining what could have been a nice evening with her.

She packed up leftovers for me to take home and walked me to the door.

"Thanks for coming. And thank you for everything you did for me this week."

"Thanks for inviting me. It was honestly one of the best meals I've ever had."

"You're welcome," she said and stared at me as if waiting for something.

"Well, goodnight," I said and turned to leave.

"Goodnight," she said with a hint of disappointment in her voice.

* * *

"I'M GOING TO GET LUNCH AT THE DELI ACROSS THE street. Do you want anything?" I asked Game, even though he'd just arrived.

"No, I ate before I came in."

"All right. I'll be back in a bit."

A few days had passed since I had dinner with Aspen, and I hadn't seen or heard from her, so I stopped by the bookstore on my way out to see if she wanted to join me for lunch.

"Hey, Coal. What are you doing here?" Josie asked.

"I wanted to see if Aspen wanted to go to lunch with me. Is she here today?"

"She is, but she already left to go to lunch. She should be back in about half an hour, but I'll tell her you stopped by."

"Thanks, Josie. Catch ya later."

I left feeling slightly disappointed and headed across the street to the deli where I had lunch at least once a week. I walked in and started for the counter to place my order when a flash of curly, red hair caught my eye. I moved to get a better look and could not believe what I was seeing.

Aspen was at the deli having lunch, and she was not alone. In fact, she was sitting with the last person I would have expected to see her with, and it was obvious by their mannerisms that they were familiar with each other.

Forgetting about my own lunch, I walked right over to their table. "I didn't expect to see you here," I said, not sure which one of them I was talking to.

"Hey, Coal," Aspen said cheerfully. "This is my stepfather, Luke. Luke, this is my friend and neighbor, Coal. Would you like to join us?"

"Your stepfather?" I asked in surprise.

"Yes," Aspen said slowly, confused by my reaction.

I turned my attention to the man sitting across from her. "Care to explain, Uncle Luke?"

"Uncle?" Aspen blurted.

Luke sighed and gestured to an empty chair at their table. "Have a seat." Then, he turned to Aspen. "I'm sorry I never told you about my family. Not talking about them is part of the job. I don't like it, but it's necessary for their safety."

"For what it's worth, I never asked," Aspen admitted.

I cleared my throat, anxious for him to explain how he had a stepdaughter none of us knew about.

"Right. So, technically, Aspen isn't my stepdaughter. I was in a relationship with her mother years ago, but we were never married."

"And you still have a relationship with her even though you don't have one with her mother?" I asked.

"It's a long story. Do you have time to hear it now?"

"I'll make time," I told him.

"I'm familiar with this story and don't need to hear it again," Aspen said and looked at the time on her phone. "And I need to get back to work," she said and all but ran for the door.

Luke exhaled slowly. "She doesn't have a good relationship with her mother. Actually, she doesn't have a relationship with her at all. It's a touchy subject for her."

"I'm starting to see that. So, what happened?"

"I met Aspen's mother, Pamela, years ago while I was working on a case. She actively pursued me, and our relationship progressed rather quickly. We'd been seeing each other for a few months when the lease on my rental house was up for renewal. She asked me to move in with her, saying it'd really help her out since things were tough for her as a single mother. Since my job kept me away more often than not, I didn't think living together would change much, so I agreed. I didn't know until two years later that the whole thing was a ruse. Pamela was working for the man I was investigating. By eavesdropping on my conversations, snooping through my phone and emails, and having access to my schedule, she was able to give him all the information he needed to stay one step ahead of us."

"How did you find out?"

Luke smiled sadly. "Aspen. Pamela and I didn't have a great relationship, nor did Pamela and Aspen, but Aspen and I did. She was a great kid, and it was impossible not to love her. She thought her mother was cheating on me and didn't know how to tell me. So, one night, she pretended to lock her keys in her car at work. She called me and asked if I could go by the house and bring her spare keys to her. I was in town on overnight surveillance with my partner but was able to leave long enough to get her keys. When I got to the house, I noticed the car parked in the driveway was the same one I'd been watching for months. Then, I saw the man himself in my living room having a heated conversation with Pamela. I listened outside the window until I heard enough to call for backup. We arrested both of them when my partner arrived. Then, as soon as I had a chance, I took the spare keys to Aspen. When I told her what happened, that her mother had been arrested, she confessed to lying about locking her keys in her car. Since I knew Pamela would be facing prison time, I bought the house we were living in and negotiated a shorter sentence for Pamela in exchange for custody of Aspen."

"So you own the house she lives in now?" I asked.

"Yes. I kept it after she moved out so she'd always have a place to live if she needed one."

"That explains why we've never seen anyone there."

"What do you mean?"

"Game and I live in the house directly behind her. Our backyards share a fence. You'd know that if you ever bothered to visit me."

"I would have if you'd bothered to invite me," he countered.

"Fine," I grumbled. "We both suck."

"I feel a little better knowing you and Game are close by."

"Why? Is there a reason to be worried?"

He shook his head. "No, I don't think so. Pamela's in the wind, but I doubt she knows Aspen's back in town. Even if she did, there's no reason for her to bother her."

"I wondered how she got a job at the bookstore."

Luke shrugged. "She needed a job, and we needed the help. Being able to keep an eye on her was an added bonus."

"On that note, I need to get back to work myself," I said and got to my feet. "But one more thing before I go. When are you telling Mom?"

Luke grimaced. "I'll call her tonight."

"Good luck with that. Let me know how it goes."

7

ASPEN

As soon as I got off work, I went over to the gym to talk to Coal. I wanted to explain why I hadn't told him about my mother. Assuming he'd still talk to me after his lunch with Luke.

I entered the gym and went to the front desk to ask for Coal, but no one was there. As I was waiting, a guy in workout clothes and a busted-up face walked over to me. His eyes ran over my body, and he came to a stop far too close for my liking. "Can I help you with something, sweetheart?"

"Is Coal here?" I asked and took a step back.

He stepped forward and leaned closer. "No. But I am."

I tried to move away from him, but he matched every step I took until my back was up against a wall. "If he's not here, I'll come back later," I said.

"What if I want you to stay?"

"What the fuck are you doing?" Game bellowed before he yanked the guy away from me.

"I was chatting with the pretty lady."

"No, you were crowding her and making her uncomfortable. Get your ass back downstairs. You aren't supposed to be up here anyway."

"Whatever, man," the guy said and walked away.

"I'm sorry, Aspen. Are you okay?"

"Yeah, I'm fine," I said, even though I was a little rattled by the interaction. "I came by to see if Coal was here."

"No, he's already gone for the day. Did you need something?"

"No, I just wanted to talk to him for a minute. It's not a big deal. I'll see you later."

I hadn't been home long when I got a text from Coal.

Coal: Heard you were looking for me.

Aspen: I stopped by to see how the rest of your lunch went.

I held my phone in my hand and waited for his reply. When it still hadn't come after several minutes, my stomach started to sink. I couldn't even begin to imagine what he thought of me after hearing what Luke had to say.

I jumped and almost dropped my phone when someone knocked on the door. I peeked out the window to see Coal standing on my front porch and quickly opened the door to let him in.

"I'm sorry I didn't tell you about my mother," I blurted as soon as I closed the front door.

"It's okay."

"It's not, but how do you tell someone your mother

is a criminal who spent years in prison, was released, and is now wanted for multiple murders? It's not exactly the best conversation starter."

"It's fine. Really," he insisted. "You didn't lie to me. You just didn't say anything about her. And honestly, the history you have with your mother is not something you should be expected to openly share, especially with someone you just met."

"You were open with me about your family history," I pointed out.

"I was, to a degree," he admitted and took a seat on the couch. "It's not a pretty story, but I'll tell you if you want to know."

"I do want to hear it, but if we're going to swap shitty stories, I'm going to need a drink," I said and held up a bottle of vodka. "I'm having Sprite Zero and vodka. Do you want one?"

He grinned. "Sure, I'll take one."

I quickly made our drinks and joined him on the couch to hear the rest of his story.

"I told you I was adopted and later reconnected with my biological family. What I didn't tell you was that I was taken from my biological mother, Annabelle, at birth and given to my adoptive family without her consent. My mother was being kept on a farm against her will. She was pregnant when she was taken, but she didn't know she was carrying twins. When she gave birth, she was told my twin died and had no idea I existed. My biological father, Phoenix, thought my mom was dead and didn't know she was pregnant when she disappeared, so he didn't know about us either."

I listened intently while he told me the whole story. "So your adoptive parents didn't know?"

"No, they were completely innocent in all of it."

"But your name," I started, unsure of how to ask without sounding like I was making an accusation.

"Obviously, the man behind everything was insane. He told my adoptive parents that my mother died shortly after delivering me and asked them to keep the name she had given me. When in all actuality, he was the one who named me. It was another one of his sick games, naming me accordingly and having me right there in front of my biological mother. I even have my biological father's middle name."

"And the crazy guy was your uncle?" I asked for clarification.

"Technically, yes. He was my biological father's half brother."

"Wow, that's…I don't even know what to say."

He nodded in agreement. "There's nothing to say. It is what it is," he said and paused. "You haven't said anything about your father. Is he in the picture?"

I shook my head. "No, he isn't and never was. He was the CEO of a company my mother worked for. He was married and having an affair with her. When he found out she was pregnant, he wanted nothing to do with her or me. She threatened to tell his wife, so he offered to pay her to keep her quiet. For years, he sent her several thousand dollars every month, until his wife discovered he was having an affair with her sister and killed him."

"Damn. We both have fucked up stories."

"I don't know whose is worse, yours or mine," I said and slapped my hand over my mouth. "I'm sorry. That sounded rude."

Coal laughed. "Maybe to someone else, but I know

what you mean. I definitely wouldn't have told you about my family if I didn't know about yours. Well, not this soon anyway."

"I'm glad you did. After I left you and Luke, I spent the rest of the day worried about what you thought of me."

"How drunk are you?" he asked, catching me off guard.

"I'm not. I've got a little buzz, but it won't last much longer without another drink. Why?"

He leaned forward and pressed his lips to mine, gently at first, but things quickly escalated until we were practically devouring each other.

Suddenly, he broke the kiss. "Does that answer your question?"

"What question?"

"What I think about you."

"Yes, I suppose it does," I said, still trying to get my bearings.

"I've been wanting to do that since you touched my scars in the hotel room," he confessed.

"Well, it sure took you long enough. I thought I'd been friend-zoned."

He laughed. "No fucking way. I've been struggling to keep my hands to myself."

"Why did you?" I asked, genuinely curious.

"You had a lot going on. I didn't want to push too hard too soon. And I didn't want you to think I expected anything from you in exchange for helping you."

"I didn't get that vibe from you at all. If anything, I thought you were tolerating me because you felt sorry for me."

"I guess we were both wrong," he said and captured my lips again.

He pulled away before I was ready and rested his forehead against mine. "As much as I'd like to stay and continue this, I have to get to the clubhouse for a meeting. Are you working tomorrow?"

"Yes," I answered, still trying to catch my breath.

"Do you want to eat lunch together?"

"Yes, I'd like that," I smiled and got up to walk him to the door.

When we stepped outside, there was a box sitting on my front porch. He picked it up and handed it to me. I glanced at the label and sighed. "Any chance you know who S.M. Gal is?"

"No, why?"

"This is the second delivery I've gotten for them. I was hoping maybe they were a neighbor and I could let them know whoever sent it has their address wrong."

"They could be. I've met a few of the neighbors, but not all of them."

"I guess I'll drop it off at the post office on my way to work in the morning and let them figure out what to do with it."

"That's what I would do," he said and leaned down to give me a quick kiss. "I'll see you tomorrow."

* * *

When I met Coal for lunch the next day, he invited me to a pool tournament the club was hosting at the bar they owned that weekend. After work on Friday, I rushed home and managed to have myself ready on time, despite changing outfits multiple times. He didn't say it was a date, but it felt like one, so I was a little nervous.

Even though we arrived at the bar an hour before the tournament was supposed to begin, the place was packed. "Is it always like this?"

"It's pretty busy on the weekends, but never like this."

I wasn't a huge fan of crowds and hoped the place was bigger inside than it looked from the outside. Being continuously bumped by strangers wasn't my idea of a good time.

I soon realized I didn't need to worry. The club had a designated VIP section for the members and their guests. Coal walked me over to a table where Game and Drew were sitting and went to the bar to get our drinks.

"Sorry it took so long," Coal said when he finally returned. "They had a bartender call in sick, and Layla's struggling to keep up with the crowd."

"I was a bartender before I moved here. Do you think she'd want my help?" I asked.

"I'm sure she would. Are you sure you don't mind?"

"I've been the only one behind the bar on a busy night before, and it sucked. I'm happy to help."

Coal escorted me behind the bar and offered my help to Layla.

"Girl, if I wasn't so busy, I'd hug you. Jump in whenever you're ready," she said.

"I'll check on you in a bit," Coal said and kissed me on the cheek before he went back to the table with Game.

"I'll be fine," I assured him and started helping customers.

It took some time, but we managed to get caught up

enough to have a steady flow of customers instead of a massive crowd surrounding the bar. Things were going smoothly, until they weren't.

It started when I looked up to find the guy from the gym, Shane, standing in front of me. "Gin and tonic, sweetheart," he said and tossed his card onto the bar. "Go ahead and make two. I'll start a tab."

I nodded and took his card, then quickly made his drinks. "Here you go."

He picked up one of the glasses and drank the whole thing before he placed the glass on the counter and winked at me. "When you see me coming, start making another."

"Yep," I said and moved to the next customer.

I'd been at it for over an hour when Coal appeared at the bar. "You doing okay?"

"Yeah," I said and handed him a beer. "It's busy, but I'm good."

Layla sidled up next to me and bumped me with her hip as she continued mixing drinks. "She's fucking phenomenal. There's no way I would've made it through tonight without her."

"Yeah, she is," Coal said and leaned over the bar to kiss me before returning to his seat.

Shortly after that, one of the waitresses, Sydney, gave me a large drink order from one of the tables she was serving. "I need seven lemon drop shots, two margaritas on the rocks, three vodka and cranberries, and two whiskey sours." I repeated it back to her to confirm the order before I started making the drinks.

She came back to pick up the drinks and scoffed. "This isn't right. It's supposed to be seven tequila shots, three margaritas, two gin and tonics, and two crown and cokes. If your fuck up costs me my tip, we're going to have problems. I don't know where you came from, but you can go back if you can't do any better than this."

"Sydney!" Layla scolded. "I heard you give her the order, and I heard her repeat it back to you, so if anyone fucked up, it's you. You need to apologize to Aspen, and then you can give your orders to me for the rest of the night."

"Sorry, Aspen," Sydney sneered and walked away.

"Don't let that bother you," Layla said. "It has nothing to do with you and everything to do with Coal."

"Great," I said slowly, suddenly feeling uncomfortable.

"It's nothing like that. She has a crush on him, but the feelings aren't mutual," she explained.

"So she's jealous?"

"Pretty much," Layla confirmed.

Then, my least favorite customer returned and demanded two more drinks. I made them and handed them over. He'd been back several times before that, and I was starting to wonder if I should continue to serve him.

When he came back the next time, there was no question in my mind. He was slurring his words and could barely hold himself upright. "Two more, bitch," he said and slammed his hand on the counter.

"I'm really sorry, but I can't serve you anymore," I said as nicely as possible. "It's not safe."

"The fuck do you mean?" he roared and pounded his fist on the bar. "I'm a paying customer, and I want my fucking drinks, bitch!"

Suddenly, Shane was on the ground, and Copper was standing over him. "She said no. Which means I said no. Now, I suggest you get up and get the fuck out of here before you find yourself in the kind of trouble you can't get out of."

Shane managed to get to his feet. "I can't leave without paying."

"I got it," Layla said and handed the card and receipt to Copper.

"Don't even think about fucking her over on the tip," Copper warned.

I flinched when I felt an arm circle around my waist from behind before I realized it was Coal. "You okay?"

"I'm fine. I just hate that I caused a scene."

"You didn't. He did. You were right to cut him off."

"Yes, you were," Layla said. "A lot of bartenders don't seem to care. I'm glad you do."

Copper returned a few moments later. "I hope that little fucker has the hangover from hell tomorrow," he grumbled.

"Did you get him in a cab?" Layla asked.

"No, one of his buddies agreed to take him home to get him out of here faster since he couldn't understand when to shut his mouth."

"We've had some issues with him at the gym, too," Coal added.

"Is he the one who kicked you?" I asked.

"That'd be him."

"He did what now?" Copper asked.

"He doesn't understand the concept of sparring. Or maybe he does and doesn't care, but he goes way too hard sometimes. He damn near broke my ribs last week," Coal explained.

"You're the one who did that to his face?" Copper asked in surprise.

"Yeah," Coal nodded. "I thought a taste of his own medicine might be more effective than talking to him."

"Nice work, man," Copper chuckled.

"I'm not sure it did any good."

"I'll touch base with Bronze tomorrow. It might be time to cut him loose," Copper said.

Coal nodded and turned to Layla. "Do you think I can have my girl back now?"

Layla grinned. "Yeah, I think I can manage on my own for the rest of the night. But, Aspen, I can't thank you enough for stepping in. I wouldn't have made it through tonight without you."

"I'm glad I could help."

"If you ever want a job here, you've got one," Layla said.

"Thanks, I'll keep that in mind."

"Are you ready to get out of here?" Coal asked.

"I'm ready if you are."

With that, we said our goodbyes and headed home.

"Other than Shane, did you have a good night?"

"Yeah, for the most part. Sydney tried to say I messed up an order, but Layla called her out on it."

"Fucking Sydney," he grumbled.

"Layla said she has a crush on you."

He sighed. "I guess that's what it is. I was nice to her one time, and she's been a pain in my ass ever since."

"How so?"

"How was I nice, or how is she a pain in the ass?"

"Both."

"She gave me a sob story one night about how her and her roommate had been arguing, and she didn't feel safe to go home. She was crying and carrying on, and I felt sorry for her. This was back when I lived with Savior.

He was rarely home, so I told her she could come home with me and sleep in the spare bedroom. He ended up coming home that night. When I was in the living room talking to him, she snuck into my room and was waiting for me in my bed. I told her in no uncertain terms to get the fuck out. I guess she thought I meant that literally because she was gone when I woke up the next morning. She's never mentioned it, and neither have I, but she relentlessly flirts with me whenever she has the chance. I've learned to completely ignore her, which is why it didn't even occur to me to mention it to you."

"How often do you see her?"

"I only see her if she's working when I stop by the bar, which isn't that often. Tonight was the first time I've been to Precious Metals in a few weeks."

My stomach chose that moment to growl. Loudly. "Sorry, I guess I'm hungry."

Coal laughed. "No need to apologize. I'm hungry too. Do you want to go get something to eat?"

"I was going to make pancakes when I got home. Do you want to join me?"

"Will there be bacon?"

"There can be."

"Then, yes, I'll join you."

"Really? Bacon was the deal breaker?"

"Of course not. I was just asking," he joked.

"Do you mind if I take a quick shower first?" I asked once we got to my house. I wanted to wash the bar off of me and get comfortable before I started the pancakes.

"Go right ahead."

"Make yourself comfortable," I said and headed for my bedroom. "I won't be long."

I pulled my hair up on top of my head and hopped

in the shower to quickly rinse off. Then, I put on a fitted long-sleeve shirt and a pair of leggings and returned to find Coal on my couch playing a game on his phone.

"When you said quick, you meant it."

"I just needed to rinse off. I always feel sticky after bartending," I said and headed to the kitchen.

"What are you doing with the bacon?" he asked when he saw me placing the strips on a cookie sheet.

"Baking it."

"Can you do that?"

I laughed. "I do it all the time. It's easier to cook, easier to clean up, and I think it tastes better this way."

"You're right. It is better this way," he said after trying baked bacon for the first time.

I smiled proudly. "Told you."

Once we were finished eating, I got up and went to the sink to rinse my plate and start cleaning up, but I soon felt Coal's presence behind me. He waited until I put the plate in the dishwasher before he turned me around and lifted me onto the counter. "I've got this," he said and took over the dishes.

"Thank you," I said sincerely after he finished washing the dishes and wiping down the counters.

He stepped between my legs and put his hands on my waist. "Thank you for cooking," he said and kissed my lips.

He started off slow but was soon kissing me with an intensity that was almost too much yet somehow not enough.

Moaning in encouragement, I wrapped my legs around his waist and buried my fingers in his hair to pull him closer.

He pulled back and met my eyes. "If we're going to do this, you're mine and no one else's."

"I don't want to be anyone's but yours."

As soon as the words left my mouth, his lips were on mine and his hands were everywhere—my legs, my ass, my back. Everywhere except where I wanted them. I ran my hands down his body and slipped them under the hem of his shirt, slowly smoothing my way up his chest to pass my hands over his nipples, hoping he'd take the hint.

He did. His lips left mine as he kissed his way to my ear. "Are you trying to tell me something?"

Yes, yes, I was, but I didn't want to say it. Instead, I answered by taking my shirt off and tossing it on the floor.

His lips crashed into mine as he quickly unclasped my bra and cupped my breasts with his large hands. I groaned in pleasure when his fingers began toying with my nipples.

His mouth left mine and moved to my breast, sucking my nipple deep into his mouth while he flicked his tongue over the hard peak. When I felt his fingers grip the waist of my leggings, I lifted my ass off the counter so he could pull them down. My underwear went with them, leaving me completely naked on my kitchen counter.

"Fuck," he growled, and then his face was between my legs devouring me.

"Oh, please, please, please," I begged. "Please don't stop."

He didn't. He continued working me into a frenzy. Then, he inserted his fingers, and I thought I was going to die right then and there.

I gripped his hair and pushed on his head. "Wait, wait, wait," I panted.

His head shot up, and his eyes were full of concern.

"You're about to make me come."

He grinned. "Yeah, that's what I was trying to do."

"I want to come while you're fucking me," I quickly explained, hoping I hadn't ruined the moment.

His grin morphed into a sly smile. "Wish granted," he said and carried me to my room.

He tossed me onto my bed and removed his shirt before he moved over me. While he sucked on my nipples, he circled my clit with his fingers before sliding them back inside me. I couldn't take much more.

"Please take your pants off and fuck me," I blurted and tried to scoot away from him.

I felt him grin against me, followed by the wonderful sound of his pants coming off.

"Condom?" I asked.

He held up one for me to see before ripping it open and rolling it down his shaft. I widened my legs, and thankfully, he didn't tease me. He lined himself up and thrust inside in one fluid movement.

"Yes!" I groaned. "Oh, fuck yes."

He moved with precision, hitting all the right spots.

"Fuck, you feel good," he said, pumping into me.

I was too far gone to formulate words. It was all I could do to hold on and enjoy the ride.

But I couldn't hold on for long. Suddenly, the orgasm that had been building reached its peak, and pleasure rippled through my body. All the while, Coal continued moving, wringing every possible ounce of pleasure from me. Then, he flipped me over, pulled my hips back as he entered me, and set to work finding his own release.

He dropped to the bed beside me, and I rolled over to face him. "That was," I started but trailed off, unable to find the right words.

"Yeah, it was," he said and gently kissed my lips.

8

COAL

After that night, Aspen and I spent most of our free time together. I couldn't get enough of her, and it seemed she felt the same way about me. Even though it'd only been a few weeks, we'd become very comfortable with one another. So much so that I'd given her a key and the alarm code to my house, and she'd given me hers.

I went to Aspen's house after work like I usually did on the days I was scheduled to close the gym. When I arrived, I walked to the front door to let myself in and saw another package sitting on her front porch.

"Special delivery," I said after closing the door behind me.

"Are you serious?" she asked in disbelief and took the box from my hands. "This is getting ridiculous."

I had to agree with her. A box addressed to S.M. Gal had shown up at her house at least four times. Each time, she returned it to the post office, then another box would show up. After the last time, she thought it might be the same package and used a blue permanent marker to color a small circle on the bottom.

"Is it the same one?" I asked.

"Yes!" she said and pointed to the blue circle. "Why do they keep sending this back to me?"

"I guess because it has your address on it."

"I've repeatedly told them it's the wrong address. I don't know what else I'm supposed to do."

I took the box from her hands and placed it on the counter so I could wrap my arms around her. "We can worry about it tomorrow. How was your day?"

"Pretty boring actually. The bookstore isn't very busy. I'm surprised they even need me."

"You don't like working there?"

"It's not that I don't like it. There's just not much to do. I'd prefer to be a little busier."

"Have you asked if they have more work for you?"

"No, but I guess I could. Enough about me. How was your day?"

"It was fine until Shane started bitching about not getting enough time in the ring. He kept on and on about it until Bronze finally sent him home. We're having a meeting about him tomorrow, but I think it's just a formality. I'm pretty sure Bronze is done with him."

"I'm sorry you had a bad day," she said and raised up on her tiptoes to kiss me. "Maybe I can make you feel better."

She took my hand and led me to the bedroom, where she did indeed make me feel better. Twice.

* * *

"COAL!" ASPEN WHISPERED URGENTLY WHILE SHAKING my shoulder. "Coal!"

"What?" I mumbled sleepily.

"Shhh! I think someone's trying to break in."

I was instantly wide awake and sat up in bed.

"I heard something out back."

"Stay here and call Game," I instructed and got out of bed. I picked up my gun from the nightstand and left the room to see what was going on.

I quietly moved through the house toward the back door, where it sounded like someone was jiggling the doorknob. The glass was covered with a frosted privacy film, but I could see the silhouette of a person on the other side.

I looked down at the door to see they'd already unlocked the deadbolt and were steadily working on the remaining lock. Moments later, the door was pushed open, and someone stepped inside.

I raised my gun and swiftly brought it down on the back of their head. The person groaned and dropped to the floor. Following them down, I pulled their hands behind their back and straddled their hips to hold them down.

"Fuck, man! Are you okay?" Game shouted as he came through the open back door.

"Hit the lights and get me something to tie their hands with."

He flipped the light switch and tossed me his belt.

I made quick work of securing their hands before I flipped the person over.

"Holy shit!" "Son of a bitch!" we said at the same time as we looked down at an unconscious Shane on Aspen's kitchen floor.

"What in the hell is he doing here?"

"I don't know, but we're going to find out. I need to go make sure Aspen's okay. You got him?"

"Yeah, man. Go ahead."

I hurried back to the bedroom to find Aspen nowhere in sight. "Aspen, baby, everything's okay."

I heard a rustling sound before she appeared from her closet. "Was someone out there?"

"Yes, but we got him."

"You what? Where? Are you okay? We need to call the police."

"Slow down. Everything's okay. He's out cold and tied up in the kitchen," I explained and paused, unsure of how she'd take the next part. "It's Shane, so I'm going to call Copper first. He'll probably want us to bring him to the clubhouse instead of calling the police."

"Okay," she said, sounding reluctant.

"Get dressed and wait in here. I'll be back in a few minutes."

I walked back to the kitchen and called Copper, grimacing when I noticed the time.

"What happened?" he asked immediately.

"Shane just broke into Aspen's house. I've got him tied up in her kitchen."

"Son of a bitch. Bring him to the clubhouse, and I'll meet you there. Is Aspen okay?"

"She's pretty shaken up."

"I'll bring Layla with me. See you in a few."

"He wants us to bring him to the clubhouse," I told Game. "But there's no way I'm making Aspen ride in the truck with him."

"Toss him in the truck bed," Game suggested.

Ten minutes later, we were on our way to the clubhouse with Aspen bundled in the front seat next to me, and Shane tied up in the bed of my truck with Game watching over him from the back seat.

Layla was waiting by the front door when we arrived. She opened her arms wide, and Aspen went right to her. "Let me make you a cup of tea while the boys handle business."

Once they were out of sight, Game and I carried Shane into church. He'd woken up somewhere along the way, but for the first time since I'd met him, he was keeping his mouth shut.

Bronze arrived a few minutes later, and he was pissed. "Boy, I was already tired of your shit, but now? Now, I'm done. Your ass is going back to Cherryfield one way or the other, but what you say next will determine the condition we send you back in. Got me?"

Shane's eyes widened with fear as he slowly nodded his head.

Bronze scoffed. "We're not going to pull it out of you. If you want to save your ass, start talking."

"I wasn't going to hurt anybody. I just wanted the box."

"What box?"

"The one that was delivered to her house. It wasn't hers, and she took it inside. I was just trying to get it back."

"You mean the packages Aspen has been getting are yours?" I asked.

"No, not exactly."

Bronze growled and smacked Shane across the face. "That's the only warning you'll get. Tell us what we need to know."

Shane inhaled deeply and dropped his head. "I guess it doesn't matter since I'm fucked anyway. The box belongs to my dealer. It's cocaine."

"Fucking hell!" I shouted. "You mean there's a box of cocaine inside Aspen's house right now?"

Shane nodded but kept his eyes focused on the floor.

"Why's it being sent to her house?"

"It's the easiest way to move it without getting caught. Have it mailed to a house no one lives at and pick it up once it's delivered."

"Who's your dealer?" Copper demanded.

"Fuck, man, don't make me do this."

Bronze slipped on a pair of brass knuckles and stepped forward. "Have it your way. I'll beat the piss out of you, and we'll still find out."

"It's Sydney!" Shane blurted.

"As in Sydney the waitress from Precious Metals?" I clarified.

"Yes. Sydney Gallagher."

"Mother fucker," Copper swore. "Is she dealing at the bar?"

"I swear I don't know. I always went to her house to get it."

Copper looked at his phone and sighed. "Let's put him in a room downstairs for the rest of the night. I'll call everyone in for church in the morning, and we'll discuss what to do about Sydney."

"Right this way, fuckwad," Bronze said and grabbed Shane's arm to hoist him to his feet. Game followed behind them, leaving me alone with Copper.

"There's something I think you should know, but I didn't want to say anything in front of Shane."

"Go ahead," Copper said.

"The house that Aspen lives in is owned by my uncle, Luke."

"You fucking serious?"

"Yes."

"So what you're saying is Sydney is having cocaine delivered to an FBI agent's house?"

"That's exactly what I'm saying."

"Holy shit. Well, this changes things."

"There's more," I hedged.

"I don't know if I want to hear any more," he grumbled.

"I honestly didn't think anything of it at first, and I still don't, but I think it's worth mentioning."

"Spit it out."

"Aspen is Pamela Perry's daughter. She's also sort of Luke's stepdaughter."

Copper closed his eyes and pinched the bridge of his nose. "Your uncle, a federal agent, was married to the woman we recently framed for murder, who happens to be the mother of your girlfriend, and you didn't think it was worth mentioning until now?" he asked, his volume gradually increasing until he was almost shouting.

"I didn't know until a few weeks ago, after I met Aspen. And they weren't married," I said and went on to tell him the story I got from Luke. "Aspen doesn't have anything to do with her mother. She doesn't like talking about her and was genuinely embarrassed when Luke told me about her. I don't know what's going on, but I do know Aspen's completely innocent."

"And you're in love with her."

His words caught me completely off guard. "I, what? I mean, we're dating."

"Oh, Coal," Copper clapped me on the shoulder and laughed. "Welcome to the club."

"Thanks, I think. So, you're not going to hold this against her?"

"I'm not thrilled about it, but it's not her fault her mother is a piece of shit. Just like it wasn't Layla's fault that her dad was. So, if you trust her, and Luke trusts her, there's no reason for me not to."

"Thanks, Copper."

"You know I'll have to tell the other brothers in church so we can decide the best way to handle the situation with Shane and Sydney."

"I know. I just don't want anyone to treat her differently."

"They won't," he promised.

I nodded and stood from my seat, ready to go find Aspen.

"I think you two should stay here tonight," he added.

"We are."

"Good. Layla and I are too. Let's go find our women. I'm beat," he said and yawned.

We found them curled up on one of the sofas in the common room talking quietly. "You ready for bed, Locks?"

"Ready when you are," Layla said and got up to go to Copper. "I'm sure I'll see y'all tomorrow. Goodnight."

"Goodnight," Aspen and I said at the same time.

"We're going to sleep here tonight," I told Aspen and led her down the hallway to my room.

"Can you tell me what happened?" she asked once we were in bed.

"That's an interesting way to ask."

"Layla mentioned that you might not be able to tell me. She explained why, and I get it. I don't like it all that much, but I do understand."

"I freaking love my aunt. She's really the best."

"Layla's your aunt?" she asked in surprise.

"Yeah. She's my biological mother's sister. I didn't tell you that?"

"No, you most certainly did not. So, Copper's your uncle?"

I laughed. "Yeah, I guess he is. How have I not put that together before now?"

"Technically, you didn't. I did," she pointed out.

I was enjoying our lighthearted moment and didn't want it to end, but I knew she wanted answers. "Whatever I tell you cannot leave this room. No matter what."

"Understood."

"Shane broke into your house because he wanted the package that keeps showing up on your front porch."

"Why? Is it his?"

"No, it's not. It's cocaine, and it belongs to the person he buys it from."

"Cocaine?" she almost shouted. "I've been driving around with it in my car! I took it to the post office! It's in my fucking house right now!"

"Which is exactly why we're sleeping here tonight."

"Then, what?"

"I honestly don't know. We're going to figure it out in the morning. But since it's Luke's house, I'm thinking they'll call him and let him handle it."

"Why in the world was someone having cocaine mailed to my house?"

"Apparently, it's pretty common to send drugs

through the mail and have them delivered to unoccupied houses for someone to pick up," I explained.

"That's crazy, and borderline genius."

"Yeah, that's what I thought too." I leaned forward and dropped a kiss on her lips. "Are you going to be able to go to sleep?"

"Yeah, I should be able to, since we're here. I think it'd be a different story if we were at my house. What about you?"

"I shouldn't have a problem now that the adrenaline's worn off."

"I'm so glad you were there," she said softly.

"Me, too."

* * *

Copper called everyone in for church and filled them in on the events that transpired overnight.

"Shane isn't an issue. We're sending him back to Cherryfield, and Lorcan can deal with him. But Sydney is another story," Copper said.

"Is she the reason the bar was raided a while back?" Judge asked.

"Probably. She was working there at the time."

"Either way, she's got to go," Batta said.

"Oh, she's definitely going to be fired and banned from all Blackwings establishments, but I think we should let Luke know she was using his house for her deliveries. Especially after what happened last night."

One by one, each brother voted in agreement with Copper's suggestion.

"Great, I'll give him a call."

"He's in town if you'd rather talk to him in person," Batta said.

"Yeah, I think that'd be better."

An hour later, Luke walked into the room where we held church with a look of concern on his face. "What's going on?"

Copper filled him in, and he didn't look as shocked as I'd expected. Except for the part about me being at Aspen's house when Shane broke in.

"Aspen's here?" Luke clarified.

"Yes, she's in my room."

"And the box is still at the house?"

"Yes. On the kitchen counter, I believe."

He exhaled slowly. "I can't say much because it's an ongoing investigation, but similar deliveries have been discovered in the area. I'll go by the house and get the box as soon as I leave here. If it matches the other ones we've confiscated, I'll be able to get an arrest warrant issued for Sydney. This might be the break in the case we've been waiting for. Any chance you can hold off on firing her so she doesn't get spooked and disappear?"

"Yeah," Copper said reluctantly. "I suppose we can hold off for a few days, but I don't want to keep her around much longer than that."

"Understood. I just need a little time to make sure everything's in order," he said and turned his attention to me. "I don't want Aspen at the house alone until I get this sorted. Am I right to assume you two are together?"

I nodded. "We are. I'll talk to her, but I don't think she'll have a problem staying at my place for a few days."

"Let me know if she does."

"Do you think she's in danger?" I asked. I was a little

concerned about possible retaliation, but Luke's worry amplified mine.

"No, not really, but you can never be too careful. Plus, Carter Perry was released from jail yesterday. He's hell-bent on proving his innocence, and I don't want him bothering Aspen."

"Does he even know about her?" I asked.

"If he doesn't, I'm sure he will soon. He's hired one of the best private investigator firms in the area. If there's something to find, they'll find it."

"Aspen doesn't have anything to hide."

"I know she doesn't. I just meant they'd know about Pamela's daughter, and that she recently moved back to Devil Springs."

"Gotcha."

"All right, fellas, I'll be in touch," Luke said and shook Copper's hand before leaving.

9

ASPEN

"How did it go?" I asked when Coal returned from his meeting.

"Good. They decided to bring in Luke. He's on his way to your house right now to pick up the package."

"What did he say when you told him it was cocaine?"

"He actually wasn't too surprised. He said they'd been investigating similar deliveries in the area."

"So, he thinks this is part of something bigger?" I asked.

"He couldn't say for sure, but maybe. He did say he thought you should stay at my place for a few days, and I agree."

"Should I be worried? Is someone going to come after me?" I asked, wondering what in the hell I had gotten myself into.

"It's just a precaution until he makes an arrest, which might take a few days. It's possible someone else might try to come get the box during that time."

"I don't have a problem staying with you, but I need

to go by there to get some clothes and a few other things."

"We'll go get your stuff once Luke is finished over there," he said. "He also asked me to tell you that your mother's stepson is out of jail and is trying to clear his name. He wanted me to let you know there's a possibility he, or one of the private investigators he hired, might approach you."

"What? Why? I don't know anything."

"I know that, and you know that, but he doesn't," he explained. "You don't have to talk to him if you don't want to."

I sighed. "Yeah, I do have to talk to him. If I don't, it'll look like I'm hiding something. I have no stake in my mother's guilt or innocence, or his for that matter."

* * *

IF COAL HADN'T WARNED ME, I WOULD'VE BEEN FREAKED out to find a man standing in the parking lot near my car when I left work two days later. Even though I'd never seen him before, I knew who he was.

"Are you Aspen White?" he asked and started to come closer.

"Yes, and you are?"

"Carter Perry," he introduced. "Do you know who I am?"

I did, but I acted like I didn't. "No, should I?"

"Your mother was married to my father."

"That's news to me. I don't have a relationship with my mother."

"Is that so?"

"Yes, it is. Is there something I can help you with?"

"Is there something you can help me with?" he repeated in a mocking tone. "Yes, you can tell me everything you know about her."

"I just told you I don't have a relationship with her. I haven't spoken to her since I was sixteen years old. Whatever you think I know, I can assure you, I don't."

"Your mother killed my father for his money. Your mother framed me for kiddie porn. Your mother hired a woman to pretend to be my girlfriend to plant the evidence. The same woman who was involved in an attempted kidnapping. A kidnapping that she made my son help her with. A kidnapping that happened to be of a child that belongs to a member of your boyfriend's club. Then, that same fucking night, the woman is found floating face down in your mother's pond, and my son has been missing since. And you expect me to believe you don't know anything?" he shouted.

It took a moment for his words to register. *A child that belongs to a member of your boyfriend's club.* Which child? And was he saying the Blackwings had something to do with his son's disappearance or the woman's death? Or both?

I looked at him with utter confusion written all over my face. "What?"

"You really didn't know?"

"I told you I didn't know anything," I said distractedly as his words played over and over in my head. Coal hadn't told me about an attempted kidnapping, but that didn't mean it was because he was hiding something, like a murder and a missing person.

"I can see that," he said and started to turn to leave. "You might want to consider the company you keep. It's not fun getting blamed for something someone else did."

When I got to Coal's house, I went straight to his

room and closed the door. He wouldn't be home for a few hours, but Game would be home any minute, and I needed time alone to think.

After a short nap and a long bath, I figured the best thing to do was to tell him what Carter said and flat out ask him if there was any truth to it. I wasn't worried about Coal lying to me. I had a feeling he'd be honest. I just hoped it would be something I could accept.

The moment he saw my face, he knew something was wrong. "What happened?"

"Carter Perry was waiting for me when I got off work," I started and noticed Coal's body slightly tense.

"How did that go?"

I ignored his question and asked my own. "He said my mother hired a woman to pretend to be his girlfriend to plant evidence to frame him. Then, he said that woman and his son kidnapped a Blackwings kid. He said the woman was found dead later that night, and his son is still missing. He said it in a way that made it sound like your club was involved. Do you know what he's talking about?"

He sat down on the end of the bed and sighed. "Yeah, I do. Last year, right after Thanksgiving, a man tried to kidnap Brinkley. He grabbed her out of her mother's arms in the parking lot. Bear stopped him, but the guy got away. That guy was Carter's son, Sean. Carter's girlfriend, Mitzie, is also Mackenzie's mother and Brinkley's grandmother. She told Sean they could use Brinkley to get ransom money from us and that Mackenzie knew what was going on. Mackenzie didn't know. So what Sean thought was a staged kidnapping was a real one, and Mitzie wasn't planning on using her for ransom. She planned to take Brinkley to your mother so she could take *pictures* of her."

"What kind of pictures?"

"The kind Carter says she used to frame him."

"Oh, gross," I said as my stomach churned with disgust. "Is Brinkley okay?"

"She is now. She broke her arm when Bear tackled the guy running away with her. Other than that, she seems fine. I think she was too young to understand what happened."

"What happened to Mitzie and Sean?"

"Are you sure you want to know?" he asked.

"Yes," I said, even though I didn't necessarily want to know. It was more of a need to know.

"Sean is the one who put Mitzie in your mother's pond before he skipped town."

"How do you know that and Carter doesn't?" I asked.

"That I can't answer," he said carefully.

I pressed my lips together and nodded. I didn't know what to say. I believed him, but I also knew he was leaving something out.

He leaned over and kissed my forehead, lingering for several seconds. "I'll give you some time to think."

"Carter said I should be careful of the company I keep. That it's not fun to get blamed for something someone else did. What do you think he meant?"

"He was just in jail for something he claims he didn't do. If he thinks we had something to do with Mitzie's death and Sean's disappearance, he was implying the same thing could happen to you. But he'd be wrong. For one thing, all of this happened before you moved back to Devil Springs."

"Yeah, I guess that makes sense."

"Did he say anything else?"

"No. As soon as he realized I didn't know what he was talking about, he left."

We sat in silence for a few minutes before he asked, "Do you want me to go?"

"No, not really. I'm not mad or anything. I just didn't like being caught off guard, especially about something so significant. But I don't want to talk about it anymore."

He moved closer and took me in his arms. "Are you ready for bed?"

"Yeah, I think so. It's been a long day."

"I'm going to take a shower, and then I'll join you."

When he returned, he got into bed beside me, and I snuggled against his chest. "Goodnight," he said and gently kissed my lips.

I returned his kiss and threaded my fingers through his hair, needing more. Rolling me onto my back, he removed my shirt while I took off my leggings and underwear.

He raised my arms above my head and told me to keep them there. Then, he lowered his mouth to my breast and cupped the other with his hand. He alternated between my nipples until I was begging for more. "Please, Coal."

He trailed kisses down my stomach until he reached my clit. When he flicked his tongue out and licked me, my hips bucked, and I moaned at the sensation. He slipped two fingers inside me and started slowly thrusting them in and out as his tongue moved against me. Within mere moments, he had my body shaking with an orgasm.

I was still pulsing with pleasure when he entered me. I wrapped my arms around him and clung to him while he moved, slowly at first. When he picked up the pace, the pleasure started building, and before long, I was climaxing again, bringing him over the edge with me.

"That was," I started and tried to catch my breath. "I've never had two before."

He grinned proudly. "We'll have to try for three next time."

I laughed. "I don't know if I can handle three."

"There's only one way to find out."

* * *

THE NEXT EVENING, COAL AND I WERE WATCHING A NEW reality TV show I'd recently discovered when Luke called to see if he could stop by.

He arrived a short time later and joined us in the living room. "Sydney was arrested earlier today," he said. "We were able to connect her to three delivery sites based on evidence we found during the search of her home."

"Who was she working for?" Coal asked.

"We don't know yet. She lawyered up the moment she was in handcuffs."

"Does that mean I can go home now?" I asked.

"You don't have to sound so excited about it," Coal teased.

"It's not that. If I'm going to keep staying here, I need to do laundry and pick up some more clothes," I explained. I enjoyed staying at Coal's house, but all of my belongings were at my house, and I wanted to have access to them.

"Yes, you can go home," Luke said. "But you have to remember to set the alarm."

I wasn't used to having an alarm system, and I kept forgetting to set it. But after Shane tried to break in, I knew I wouldn't forget again. Because if Coal hadn't been there, things could have turned out much differently. "I don't think that will be a problem anymore," I said.

"Good," he said. "How are things going at the bookstore?"

I opened my mouth to say, "Fine," but hesitated, and he noticed.

"You're bored," he said knowingly.

"Maybe a little," I confessed. "I don't want to complain. I needed a job, and you gave me one, no questions asked. But, yeah, I do wish I had more to do."

Luke cleared his throat. "The bookstore isn't really a bookstore. Well, it is, but its main purpose is to provide a place for agents to conduct business without drawing any unwanted attention. There's more to it than that, but if you're interested, we could definitely use some help with the administrative side of things."

"I'm definitely interested."

"You'll have to sign a nondisclosure agreement and a few other things. We'll get the paperwork completed and submitted this week so you can start your new role on Monday."

"Thank you!" I said excitedly. "I can't wait."

10

ASPEN

I'd had an uneasy feeling all day. At first, I thought I was nervous about my new role at the bookstore, but the more I thought about it, I didn't think that was the reason. I couldn't put my finger on it, but something felt off. I tried my best to ignore it, but the feeling seemed to grow stronger as the day progressed. Even with more work to do, the day seemed to drag on forever, which only made things worse. When it was finally time for me to leave, I was more than ready to get out of there and take solace in the comfort of my own home.

As I was gathering my things, my phone dinged with a text message.

Game: Is Coal with you?

I frowned at the message as my heart started to speed up. Something had to be wrong. Coal was supposed to be at work with Game. And Game wouldn't be asking about Coal if he was at work.

For a brief second, I tried to convince myself that he was probably just running late. But Coal didn't run late. And if he did, he called to let someone know.

I tried to remain calm instead of going into full-on panic mode like I wanted to and replied back to Game.

Aspen: No. I thought he had to work today.

My whole body flinched when my phone started ringing in my hand with Game's name on the screen.

"Hello," I answered and squeezed my eyes shut, bracing for whatever he was about to say.

"Hey, Aspen," Game said, sounding much calmer than I expected. "Coal was supposed to be here about an hour ago. I've tried calling him, but he's not answering his phone. When was the last time you talked to him?"

"This morning before I left for work. Do you think something's wrong?" I asked, even though I was already sure it was. I hadn't known Coal for that long, but I'd been around him enough to know that he always had his phone on him.

"I hope not, but this isn't like him," Game said, verbalizing my own thoughts.

"I'm getting ready to leave work now. I'll stop by your house and see if he's there. Maybe he got sick or fell asleep," I suggested.

"Thanks, Aspen. Let me know one way or the other."

"Same goes for you. Call me as soon as you hear from him. Or have him call me." I didn't bother to hide the desperation in my voice. Coal had quickly become a very important part of my life. The thought of something happening to him was almost too much to bear.

"Will do. Talk to you soon," Game said and ended the call.

I reached into my purse and grabbed my keys. "I'm heading out," I announced to Tatum and Josie as I headed for the back door.

"See you tomorrow," Josie called.

As I hurried to my car, millions of thoughts raced through my mind. Where could he be? What could have happened to him? Was he sick? Did he have a wreck? Maybe he slipped in the shower.

I frantically clicked the unlock button on my key fob and yanked the door open to climb inside. As I was preparing to race toward his house, it dawned on me that I was in love with Coal. I knew I cared about him deeply, but I didn't realize how much until I was faced with the possibility of losing him. The pain in my chest deepened, threatening to take my breath away, as tears started to blur my vision. I quickly blinked them away, willing myself to hold it together at least until I reached his house.

I turned the key in the ignition and started to put my car in drive when the passenger door opened. My mother got into the passenger seat and pointed a gun at my face. "Drive," she demanded.

I was too stunned to do anything but stare at her for a few seconds. "What the hell are you doing in my car?"

"I said drive!" she yelled and pressed the barrel of the gun into my cheek.

I peeled out of the parking lot and turned onto the road.

"Why are you doing this?"

"That's not for you to worry about. Just do as I say, and don't make this any harder than it needs to be."

"What do you want me to do?"

"Drive to the highway and head north," she instructed and tapped my cheek with the gun.

"Then what?"

"I'll tell you when you need to know. Until then, just drive. And don't do anything stupid, or you and your boyfriend will regret it."

Her words sent my internal panic to a new level. I was right. Something was wrong. And she was behind it.

When I came to a red light, I briefly closed my eyes and inhaled deeply, trying to calm myself. I needed to keep a level head and try to figure out how to get away from her and find Coal.

"What did you do to him?" I managed to ask.

"Just keep your mouth shut and drive."

I did as she said and continued to drive in silence. Part of me was grateful that I didn't have to hear her voice, but the other part of me wanted to demand an explanation from her and beg her not to hurt Coal. The only comfort I had was knowing Game was expecting a call from me. I knew he would alert the masses when he couldn't find me or Coal.

We'd been on the road for over an hour when she told me to take the next exit. "Look for a gas station on the right. You're going to turn onto the road beside it and drive for half a mile or so until you see a dirt road on the left. Take the dirt road and stop when your car is no longer visible from the road."

"Okay," I said quietly and glanced in the rearview mirror as I exited the highway. We were in the middle of nowhere, and there were absolutely no cars around.

I found the dirt road with ease and came to a stop when I could no longer see the road. I assumed if it wasn't visible to me, then my car wouldn't be visible from the road, but I didn't think it mattered all that much since I hadn't seen a single vehicle for miles.

"Now what?" I asked and put the car in park.

When I turned to look at her, her lips formed into a cruel smile. Before I could utter another word, she raised the gun and slammed it into the side of my head. I tried to fight back, but the first hit stunned me, making it impossible to defend myself in time. I felt her hit me two more times before everything went black.

* * *

I WOKE UP FEELING LIKE DEATH. MY HEAD WAS HURTING in a way it never had before, and there was a burning pressure in my chest. I slowly opened my eyes, only to be met with darkness.

When I put my hands down to push myself to a sitting position, I felt dirt and rocks beneath my fingers and realized I wasn't at home in my bed. I was outside on the ground somewhere and had no recollection of how I'd gotten there.

I tried to feel around for my phone, but even the smallest movements made my head pound in agony. I was so cold, and everything hurt. I just wanted to curl up into a ball and go back to sleep. But something told me not to. Something was terribly wrong; I just didn't know what. But I did know I couldn't stay where I was. I needed to get up and find help.

With the little bit of strength I could muster, I managed to get to my feet and immediately felt like I was going to fall over. It was so dark I could barely make out any of my surroundings. I tried to listen for anything that would give me a clue as to where I was or which way to go, but all I heard were the sounds of nature. There were no car engines in the distance or the buzzing of nearby homes.

I didn't know which way to go or how far I'd have to walk to find help, but I knew I had to at least try. I couldn't stay where I was and wait for someone to find me. Surely, someone was looking for me, right? But who? Why couldn't I remember anything?

Trying to remember what happened to me made my head hurt more than it already did. So, I focused my attention on trying to walk and ignored the painful protests of my body.

Thankfully, my legs seemed to work just fine, even though the pain in my head and chest was almost unbearable. It hurt to breathe. So much so that I'd grimace and tense with pain each time I inhaled too deeply. Then, my head would throb. It was a vicious cycle.

One such instance was so bad I had to brace myself against a tree while I vomited. I knew if I let myself hit the ground I wouldn't have the strength to get up again. And I refused to die alone in the woods.

I took a few minutes to recover before I forced myself to continue walking. I don't know how long it took, but it felt like an eternity had passed by the time I came to a paved road.

The sight should have brought me some relief, but I hadn't heard a car the entire time I was walking. Which meant the likelihood of finding help close by wasn't very high.

I carefully turned my head from left to right, trying to decide which way to go. From what little I could see, neither way looked promising. I didn't have the time or energy to consider my options and formulate a well thought out plan. Instead, I went with my gut instinct and turned right onto the road.

I still couldn't see shit, but it was much easier to walk on the paved road versus the dirt path I'd just been on. Still, there were so many times I wanted to give up and let the pain consume me. Sometimes it was so intense I thought my head was going to explode. And part of me wanted it to so I could get some relief. My chest felt like it was on fire, but it was nothing compared to my head.

Somewhere along the way, I started counting. Each time I made it to ten, it was like a little victory. Then, I'd start over again and focus on making it to ten. It was the only way I could make myself keep going. "Just make it to ten," I told myself over and over again.

I'd just finished another count when I saw something in the distance. It was hard to make out, and there was a chance my eyes were playing tricks on me, but it looked like there was a clearing up ahead.

I tried not to get my hopes up, but as I got closer, I could clearly see a building and an intersection.

Picking up the pace as much as I could, I finally stumbled into the empty parking lot of a gas station that had seen better days. However, my relief was short-lived when I peeked through the front door. The shelves were bare, and it looked like the place hadn't been open for quite some time. Even though I'd reached some sort of civilization, I was still alone with no way to call for help.

I considered huddling in the doorway and waiting until morning to continue, but the relentless pain in my head made the decision for me. Whatever was going on with my head was bad, and I needed to get to a hospital sooner rather than later. So, I forced myself to continue walking, and counting, vowing to keep going until I absolutely couldn't.

I wanted to cry when my eyes landed on a highway overpass in the distance. It didn't matter that I was in the middle of nowhere in the middle of the night, there would be cars on the highway. There had to be. That thought was enough to push me forward for what I hoped would be the last leg of my journey. I'd already suffered through hours of hell. Surely, I could hang in there long enough for someone to pass by.

I didn't bother looking at the signs or trying to decide which would be the best way to go. I turned onto the ramp closest to me and made my way to the highway.

I hadn't given much thought as to who would come to my rescue, and suddenly I wished I had. I assumed it would be a nice family in a minivan, or maybe even a police officer. What I didn't expect was for a gruff man on a motorcycle to pull up beside me and shut off his engine.

He remained seated on his bike and studied me for a few moments. "You okay?" he asked, even though it was obvious I wasn't.

"N-no, I'm not," I stammered, finding it hard to speak. "I'm hurt and need to go to the hospital."

"I can take you. Do you think you can ride?"

"I-I, um," I started. I didn't know if I could ride or not. I was barely able to stand at that point.

"How about I call for an ambulance to come get you?" he suggested.

"Yes, please," I said as tears began to stream down my face. "Thank you."

While he made the call, I carefully lowered myself to the gravel and cradled my head in my hands. Moments later, something warm was draped around my shoulders. I opened my eyes to see he'd wrapped his leather jacket around me.

"Thank you," I said again. "I'm so cold."

He nodded in acknowledgment. "You're going to be okay. The ambulance is on the way."

When I didn't respond, he cleared his throat. "The lady on the phone told me I should keep you talking," he said and gestured to me with his hand. "Since you have a head injury."

"How'd you know that?" I asked, slightly confused. Had I told him about my head?

"Uh, the dried blood on your face was my first clue."

"Oh," I said, somewhat surprised. It hadn't occurred to me that I might be bleeding. I raised my hand and carefully ran my fingers over my forehead. "I didn't realize I was bleeding."

"Can I ask what happened to you?"

"I don't know," I confessed. "I woke up out there somewhere," I said and gestured behind me, "but I can't remember anything."

"That's okay," he soothed. "Let's just worry about getting you to the hospital."

"Thank you for stopping. I don't know how long I've been out here, but I don't think I would've been able to keep going much longer."

"I hate to say it, but you're probably right about that. Looks like you're in pretty rough shape."

"It certainly feels like it. My head has never hurt this bad before."

"It shouldn't be too much longer before the ambulance gets here, and you can get some relief."

Thankfully, he was right. The ambulance arrived a few minutes later. While I was relieved to see them coming, the lights and siren sent my splitting headache to an entirely different level.

I thanked the man again and returned his jacket before the paramedic helped me into the back of the ambulance. Once inside, I collapsed onto the stretcher and told her what I could recall as they whisked me away to the hospital.

"Do you have any other injuries that you're aware of? Besides your head?" she asked.

"My chest hurts, and it's kind of hard to breathe, but I don't know why."

"Let me help you with your jacket, and we'll take a look."

As soon as she unzipped my jacket, her eyes widened in shock. "You've been shot," she blurted and reached for a handful of supplies.

"What?" I shouted and immediately looked down at my chest, causing a sharp pain to shoot through my skull.

I squeezed my eyes shut and rested my head against the world's worst pillow, willing myself not to vomit all over the nice woman trying to help me.

She urgently shouted something to the person driving before returning her attention to me. "I'm going to cut your shirt off so I can get a better look at your wound."

"Whatever you need to do," I said sluggishly. I could feel myself fading quickly. I'd used every bit of energy I had to get myself to the highway, and I didn't have a single drop left. Knowing I was in good hands, I closed my eyes and drifted into the darkness.

11

COAL

I knew something was wrong before I opened my eyes. My head hurt, my arms and legs hurt, and I felt extremely groggy.

I listened for a few minutes, trying to figure out what was going on, but I was met with complete silence. The only thing I could hear was an occasional breeze outside.

Assuming I was alone, I opened my eyes and slowly raised my head to take in my surroundings. But it was when I tried to move my arms that I realized the severity of my situation. I was tied to a chair with my arms secured behind my back.

The chair was situated in the middle of a dark room I presumed to be a basement based on the concrete floor, unfinished walls, and lack of windows. The only light I had was what was seeping in from the cracks around the door.

I wiggled in my seat, careful to make as little noise as possible, and tested my restraints. The ropes around my wrists were secure and didn't have any give, but the ropes around my lower legs were tied over my motorcycle boots and slightly loose. I immediately started working on getting my boots off in hopes of freeing my legs. It took much longer than I cared to admit, but I finally managed to toe off my boots and slip my legs through the ropes.

Then, I set to work on freeing my hands. I could feel the knot with my fingers, but I couldn't get a good enough grip to work on loosening it.

I considered taking my chances and trying to make a break for it with the chair still attached to me, but I didn't know what was waiting for me on the other side of the door and thought it would be best to have full use of my hands in case I needed to defend myself.

Instead, I pushed to my feet and slowly walked around the room, feeling along the walls for anything that might help me.

Unfortunately, the only thing I came across was a rough spot on the wall where a jagged piece of brick protruded. It wasn't going to be quick, and I was certain it would be somewhat painful, but I was pretty sure it was sharp enough to cut through the rope if I tried hard enough.

The spot was too high on the wall for me to sit while I worked the ropes against it and too low for me to stand comfortably. So, I was forced to bend at an awkward angle and spend what had to be hours rubbing the bindings against the sharp piece of wall.

When I heard the sound of the rope finally starting to break, a sense of relief surged through me. But I refused to acknowledge it until my hands were completely free. Because that was only part of the battle. I still had to find my way out of the room and whatever building I was in. Then, I had to get back to my family.

If they didn't find me first. I had no idea how long I'd been gone, or what had happened to me for that matter, but I knew they would be looking for me the moment they realized I was missing. With any luck, that would have been shortly after I didn't show up at work. I never missed work unless I was sick, and everyone knew it.

What I couldn't figure out was why I had been taken or who might be behind it. The club wasn't involved in any disputes, and we didn't have any enemies that I was aware of. Neither chapter did. That's not to say we hadn't in the past, but those issues had been done and over with for quite some time.

There was nothing going on in my personal life that would have warranted a kidnapping, so I was at a complete loss as to why I was taken. The only possible reason I could come up with was that someone was holding me for ransom, but who in the hell would be stupid enough to think they could kidnap the president's son and get away with it?

As I continued rubbing the rope against the wall, I tried to remember what happened. The last thing I could recall was getting ready for work. I took a shower, got dressed, and walked out to my truck. Then, nothing.

My heart pounded in my chest at the thought of Aspen being in danger. But she was at work at the bookstore when I was taken, so she had to be safe. Plus, the club would have moved her to the clubhouse once they realized I was missing. There was no need to worry about her.

But a niggling feeling told me otherwise. And that

feeling had me rubbing my bound hands faster and harder against the wall. It hurt. A lot. But I didn't relent. Not when I felt my skin start to tear from the friction and not when blood started trickling down my fingers. I didn't care what I had to do. Even if I had to cut my own hands off to get out of there and get to her.

Finally, I cut through the rope, but it didn't fall to the floor and free me instantly like I'd hoped. I had to stretch my fingers to their absolute limit while wiggling my raw wrists to unwind it.

Once I was free, I quickly put my boots on and checked my pockets to see if by chance I still had my phone or anything I could use to escape, like the pocket knife I always carried with me. As I suspected, my pockets were completely empty. At least I still had my cut.

When I was growing up, my mom would tell me to find something positive whenever I was in a bad situation. Having my cut was it. Because it reminded me that I wasn't alone. I knew I wouldn't have been alone even if it was gone, but I was clinging to the symbolism like a lifeline.

Taking a deep breath, I moved to the door and closed my eyes as I reached for the handle, silently praying it was unlocked.

In any other circumstance, a locked door wouldn't have been an issue for me. I was great with locks, when I had my tools to pick them, which I usually did. But with my pockets empty, I was on my own.

I couldn't contain the smile that spread across my face when I turned the knob, and the door opened with ease. Whoever took me either overestimated their skills or underestimated mine. It was unfortunate for them, but wonderful for me.

Stepping out of the room, I paused once again to listen for any indication that I wasn't alone. When I was sure I hadn't heard anything, I cautiously proceeded forward until I came to a set of stairs, which seemed to be the only way out.

Hoping luck would be on my side once again, I reached for the door handle and gave it a turn. I struggled to contain my growl of frustration when I found it to be locked.

"Shit," I whispered and slowly descended the stairs to look for something I could use to get the door open.

Unlike the room I'd been in previously, the main part of the basement wasn't empty. Feeling along the wall as I made my way around the room, I found a light switch and flipped it on. The overhead lights flickered to life, illuminating the room and allowing me to see clearly for the first time in hours.

I walked over to a stack of boxes and started searching. After digging through several boxes, I found a screwdriver. I'd hoped to find a pry bar, but the screwdriver would have to do.

The lock on the door was nothing special, just a standard lock one would find on an interior door of a home. I removed the screws holding the knob in place, followed by the knob, and manually moved the locking mechanism to the unlocked position. Then, I quietly eased the door open. It only opened an inch before the chain lock on the other side stopped it.

By that point, I was done with obstacles. My frustration boiled to an all-time high, and any concern I had of not being alone went out the proverbial window. I gripped the screwdriver tightly in my hand, raised my booted foot, and kicked the door open in one swift motion.

The door crashed into the wall behind it and echoed through the house. If anyone was in the house, they would know I was free. I didn't wait around to see if anyone was coming. I really didn't want to stab someone with the screwdriver if I didn't have to. I certainly would. I just didn't want to.

All I wanted to do was get home and make sure Aspen was okay. Nothing else mattered to me at that moment.

The main part of the house was dark and silent, leading me to believe I was indeed alone. But I still proceeded with caution. Someone had already gotten the drop on me, and I'd be damned if it was going to happen again.

Moving quickly through the house, I opened the first exterior door I came to and stepped outside, jogging to the nearby trees for cover. Then, I took a moment to look around. I had no idea where I was, and nothing looked familiar.

The house was actually a cabin, situated in a clearing surrounded by trees.

"Fucking great," I mumbled to myself. I couldn't see any lights in the distance or hear anything that indicated other people were nearby. Which meant I was likely at someone's remote mountain retreat.

With no idea which way to go, I picked a direction and started walking. I wanted to get moving while I had the advantage of adrenaline coursing through me. I'd consider resting once I'd put more distance between me and the cabin.

I had to have been walking for hours when I came across a creek. For all I knew, I could have been wandering around in circles since I didn't have anything to use as a point of reference. With the creek as my new guide, I continued on beside it, hoping it would lead me in the right direction.

It wasn't long before I realized I was gradually descending. Tennessee was full of mountains, and remote cabins were plentiful, to say the least. But going down a mountain didn't automatically mean I was headed toward civilization. I could just as easily be heading into a valley or ravine. But following the creek was my best option, so that's what I did.

I walked until sunlight began to fill the sky. I'd wanted to take a break many times over the past few hours, but I'd convinced myself to keep going until the sun rose, hoping I'd be able to recognize something in the daylight. And I was sorely disappointed when I didn't.

Defeat and exhaustion were starting to set in, no matter how hard I tried to keep them at bay. My wrists were covered in dried blood and ached constantly. I was beyond thirsty, and I still had a dull headache, likely from whatever was used to knock me out. Even still, I wasn't at the point where I was willing to risk drinking water from the creek. If I got desperate, I would, but I felt like I could hold out a bit longer.

When the next round of exhaustion hit, I thought of my family and how worried they must be. I told myself it would be wrong to rest knowing they were out searching for me.

I'd been gone overnight, so I knew my brothers had

come together and were out trying to find me, including my brothers in Croftridge.

The thought of Shaker flying over the forest with his helicopter and spotting me brought a small smile to my face. Even though it would be almost impossible for him to spot me through the trees, the thought gave me hope.

But as the hours passed, my hope faded. I'd walked countless miles to no avail. The only thing keeping me remotely grounded was knowing I was making progress. It was hard to keep my mind from getting carried away with all the possible outcomes. Every time I started to wonder if I'd ever see another person again, I thought of Aspen and my family and refocused my energy.

I was head over heels in love with her, and I hoped she knew how much she meant to me. If she didn't, she would as soon as I got back. Because I was going to ask her to marry me as soon as I had the chance.

I wasn't worried about her saying no or that she didn't share the same feelings as me. My only concern was the timing. Our relationship had progressed quickly, and there was a chance she might think it was too soon for marriage. But I didn't think that would be the case. She was my other half, and I was hers.

I kept my eyes focused on my feet, watching where I stepped, while I thought about how I'd propose to Aspen and what our wedding would be like.

I was imagining her walking down the aisle toward me in a beautiful white dress, surrounded by our friends and family, when the sound of a voice scared the absolute shit out of me.

"Hey, man!" someone shouted from my left. "This is private property, and you're trespassing."

I turned to locate the source of the voice, and found

a man dressed in camouflage staring at me from several yards away. Oh, and he was holding a shotgun that was thankfully not pointed at me.

I held my hands up in surrender. "I'm sorry. I didn't know I was trespassing. I'm lost and have been walking through these woods since sometime last night. Is this your property?"

"Yes, it is," he confirmed.

It felt like a ton of weight had been lifted off of my shoulders. If he owned the property, he knew where we were, and more importantly, how to get out of the woods.

"If you'll show me the way to the nearest road, I'll happily remove myself from your property."

His eyes roamed over me from head to toe and came to a stop on my bloody hands.

I shrugged. "I've had a really rough day. All I want to do is get out of these woods and go home."

"Yeah, you look like you've seen better days. Follow me. My cabin's not too far away. I'm sure you've already figured out there's no cell phone reception out here, but I can drive you into town so you can call somebody."

"Thank you. Seriously. I was beginning to think I'd never find my way out."

"How long did you say you'd been out here?"

"I don't know exactly. Since sometime last night."

"How'd you wind up out here? This area's pretty remote."

"I was camping with a group of friends and got separated from the group," I lied. I wasn't going to take the chance of scaring him off by telling him I'd been kidnapped and escaped after waking up tied to a chair in an unfamiliar cabin.

"Well, shit. They probably reported you missing and are out looking for you. Hopefully, I can get you to town before I end up with a search and rescue team traipsing all over my land and scaring off the wildlife."

There was no need for him to worry, but I couldn't exactly tell him that either. "I hope so too. You're doing me a huge favor, so I certainly don't want to cause any trouble for you."

He waved his hand dismissively. "You're not causing any trouble. I just don't like people. I come out here to get away from others, not unite with them."

"I can understand that."

When we reached his cabin, I waited outside while he went inside to get his keys. He came back out and tossed me a bottle of water.

"Thank you," I said and proceeded to down the contents in one go.

"Here. Take this one too. I'll run in and grab a couple more."

"Appreciate it. I didn't realize how thirsty I was until just now."

"I bet so," he chuckled.

"I'm Jimmy, by the way. What's your name?" he asked once we were on the road.

"Coal," I said simply and didn't offer my last name.

"Are you from around here?"

Since I didn't know where we were, I just said, "I'm from Devil Springs."

He let out a low whistle. "Y'all don't have places to camp closer to home?"

"Yeah, we do, but I wasn't the one who planned this trip. I just came along with the group."

"You got any idea where you want me to take you?"

"I'm not really familiar with the area, but anywhere with a phone I can use will be fine. Well, and preferably somewhere I can wait for someone to come get me."

"I know just the place. There's a diner in town. You can use the phone and have dinner while you wait."

The thought of food made my stomach turn. I wasn't the least bit hungry and hadn't been since the whole ordeal started. Instead, I found myself fighting off bouts of nausea every time I thought about Aspen, which was more often than not. Even though I was out of the woods and well on my way home, the uneasy feeling in my gut hadn't relented. Not even a little bit. If anything, it seemed to be getting worse.

Almost thirty minutes after we left his cabin, Jimmy turned into the diner's parking lot, which was relatively empty.

"I know it doesn't look like much, but they have some of the best food you'll ever put in your mouth." He paused and gave me a serious look. "But don't go telling all of your friends. We don't want this place to become overrun with tourists and out-of-towners."

"Your secret's safe with me," I promised. As soon as I figured out where exactly I was, I had no intention of ever returning, regardless of how good the food was.

When we entered the diner, the waitress greeted Jimmy by name and started making her way over to us with a broad smile on her face. "Hey, Jimmy. I didn't expect to see you today," she cooed.

"I wasn't planning on being here today, but I found this young man lost in the woods. He needed a ride into town to use a phone, and I thought, what better place to stop than here."

She gestured to the table. "Have a seat, and I'll take your order. Then, I'll show you where the phone is."

Jimmy rattled off his order without even glancing at the menu. I, on the other hand, didn't have a clue what to order. I really wasn't hungry and didn't think I'd be able to eat even if I tried. "Do you have cheeseburgers?" I asked.

"Oh, I'm sorry, honey. If you need to look over the menu, I can come back in a few minutes," she offered.

"If you have burgers, I'll take a cheeseburger and fries."

"You're in luck. We have some of the best burgers around. What would you like to drink?"

"Sweet tea, please."

"Sure thing," she smiled. "Follow me over here, and I'll get the phone for you."

I took a seat on one of the barstools at the counter, and she placed the phone in front of me. I picked up the receiver and paused, suddenly realizing that I hadn't bothered to memorize anyone's phone number in years. I hadn't needed to since they were all stored in my cell phone.

There was one phone number I knew by heart. Uncle Luke's cell phone. He had me memorize it when I was a child in case I ever needed to call him in an emergency. Thankfully, he still had the same number all these years later.

I quickly dialed his number and held my breath while I waited for him to answer. I didn't know what I would do if he didn't.

"Luke Johnson," he barked into the phone.

"Uncle Luke," I exhaled, overwhelmed with relief at the sound of his voice.

"Coal!" he shouted. "Where are you? Are you okay?"

I cleared my throat and chose my words carefully, knowing Jimmy and the waitress were listening to my conversation. "Yeah, I'm good. I, uh, got separated from the other campers and have been lost in the woods. I ran into a hunter, and he gave me a ride into town. I called you as soon as I got here. Can you arrange for someone to pick me up?"

"You've been camping?" he asked in disbelief.

"No."

He didn't miss a beat. "Cover story?"

"Yes."

"Gotcha. Tell me where you are, and I'll get someone to you."

I moved the phone away from my mouth and made eye contact with the waitress. "Excuse me, ma'am, can you tell me the address for this place so my friend can pick me up?"

"Of course, darling," she said and rattled off the address.

I repeated it to Luke and managed to contain my surprise when she said Rockwood.

Luke, however, did no such thing. "How in the hell did you end up all the way out there? No wonder it took you so long to call. It'll be at least an hour, if not longer, but stay put. Someone will be there to get you."

"Trust me. I'm not going anywhere."

"Can I call you back at this number if I need to?" he asked.

"I don't see why not. It's the diner's business phone. I'm sure it'll be fine."

"All right. Sit tight while I make some calls."

"Can you let my parents know I'm okay? Copper and Aspen too? I don't have my phone on me, and yours was the only number I could remember."

He didn't answer immediately, and his hesitation didn't sit well with me. "Uh, yeah, I can do that."

"Thanks, Uncle Luke."

"No need to thank me, kid. I'm just glad you're okay. We'll see you soon."

I thanked the waitress again for letting me use the phone and stopped by the restroom to use the facilities and wash my hands before returning to the table.

I caught a glimpse of myself in the mirror and realized I needed to wash my face too. I had dirt and dried blood smeared across my cheeks and forehead. With the way I looked, it's a wonder Jimmy offered to help me. But I guess he didn't view me as a threat, seeing as how he had a shotgun and I didn't.

"You look like a new man," Jimmy said when I returned to the table.

"I wish I felt like one."

"I'm sure you'll feel ten times better after you get something to eat."

I disagreed but kept it to myself. I wouldn't feel any better until I was home and had Aspen in my arms.

"Were you able to get in touch with your friends?"

"I called my uncle. He's sending someone to pick me up, and he's going to let everyone else know I've been found. He did say it might take an hour or two for someone to get here. I don't want you to feel obligated to stay and wait with me, but I would like to thank you for your help by paying for your dinner."

He grinned and lowered his voice. "I don't mind

waiting. It gives me an excuse to visit with Cheryl." I briefly wondered if something more was going on between the two of them or if they just enjoyed flirting with each other.

Forty-five minutes later, my dad entered the diner like a man on a mission, followed by Dash and Shaker. He made a beeline for me as soon as his eyes landed on me, and he didn't hold back. I barely had time to get to my feet before he wrapped me up in a tight hug.

"Coal," he breathed. "You scared the shit out of me. Are you okay?"

"I've been better, but it's nothing a few days of rest won't fix," I said and forced a smile before I turned my attention to Jimmy. "Dad, this is Jimmy. He's the man who found me and gave me a ride into town."

Dad extended his hand. "I can't thank you enough. My wife and I have been worried sick since we found out he was missing."

I nonchalantly nudged him with my elbow. "I told him I'd pay for his dinner, but I don't have my wallet."

Dad turned his eyes to Dash. "Take care of that, would ya?"

"On it," he said and walked over to the counter.

"Thank you," Jimmy said, "but I was happy to help."

Dad reached into his pocket and pulled out a business card. "You saved my son's life today. If there's ever anything I can do for you, please don't hesitate to call."

Jimmy waved his hand dismissively. "Nonsense. I just helped him get found a little faster is all."

Dad chuckled. "We'll have to agree to disagree, but my offer still stands. I'll be happy to return the favor."

"I'll keep that in mind," Jimmy said and placed the card in his back pocket.

Dash returned to where we were standing. "You ready to get out of here?"

"Hell yes," I said, causing them all to laugh.

I followed them out the door and to the only other vehicle in the parking lot. "Whose is this?" I asked.

"It's a rental," Dash explained. "Shaker flew us here. While we were in the air, Luke arranged to have a rental ready and waiting for us at the airport."

"I was wondering how you got here so fast."

The moment we were all inside the car with the doors closed, Dad demanded to know what happened.

"I'm not sure. I think I might have been drugged because there's a large chunk of time I can't account for."

"That's okay. Just tell us what you can."

"I was at home getting ready to go to work. I remember walking out to my truck to leave. Then, I woke up tied to a chair in someone's basement."

"Whose basement?"

I shrugged. "I don't know. No one was there when I woke up. Once I got myself free, I didn't hang around to investigate. I got the hell out of there as fast as I could."

"Good. That was the right thing to do. Do you have any idea where you were?"

I shook my head. "It was dark when I made it out. I walked through the woods for hours until I found a creek to follow, and I didn't stop walking until about thirty minutes before I called Luke. I have no idea how far I walked or what direction I was traveling in. I'm not even sure I could find my way back to Jimmy's cabin."

"I'll call Byte and have him start digging. He should

be able to find Jimmy's cabin. Then, we can search the surrounding area until we find what we're looking for. Do you have any idea who took you?"

"No. Do you?"

"Hold that thought," Shaker interrupted. "We're here."

I waited until we were in the air to revisit my unanswered question. "Do you know who's behind this?"

Dad shifted in his seat to face me while he spoke into his headset. "No, not for sure, but we have an idea."

"Who?" I asked, wondering why he was holding back.

"Pamela Perry."

"Aspen's mother?" I asked in disbelief. "I know she's a piece of shit, but what would she want with me?"

"That's what we're trying to figure out."

"Have you talked to Aspen? What does she think about it?"

Dad's eyes closed, and he inhaled deeply. Then, he placed one hand on my shoulder and gently squeezed.

"No one has seen or heard from Aspen since she left work yesterday."

"What?" I whispered, hoping I hadn't heard him correctly even though I knew I had.

"We're doing everything we can to find her. The clubs, the police, the FBI. Everyone is searching for her. And that's exactly what we'll be doing as soon as we land in Devil Springs."

Suddenly, Luke's odd hesitation on the phone made sense. He already knew Aspen was missing, and after my call, he knew she wasn't with me.

"It'll be okay, son. We found you, and we're going to find her."

But how long would it be before we found her, and what condition would she be in when we did? The possible answers to those questions were too much for me to think about. I could barely breathe and was on the verge of completely breaking down. She couldn't be gone. She just couldn't.

"Is there anything you can think of that might be useful? Anything she might have told you about her mother?" Dash asked.

"Aspen hates her mother. She hasn't spoken to her in years. What makes you think Pamela is behind this?"

"Luke's team used footage from traffic cameras to try and track Aspen's car. Before you get your hopes up, they lost her on the highway once she was out of city limits. But, in one of the images they did get, you can see someone in the passenger seat, and Luke said that person matched Pamela's description."

I closed my eyes and rubbed my forehead, trying to put the pieces together. "None of this makes any sense. There's no way Pamela could have taken me, dumped me in a basement in the middle of nowhere, and been back in Devil Springs by the time Aspen got off of work."

"We think someone's helping her," Dad suggested.

That made more sense. "Any idea who that could be?"

"No, not yet, but with the amount of people working on this, we should know sooner rather than later."

"I'd really rather they focus their efforts on locating Aspen and worry about who was behind it later."

"I know, son. If anyone understands how you feel,

it's me. But we need to know who's behind this so we know where to look. Otherwise, we're searching for a needle in a haystack."

"Yeah, I guess you're right," I admitted and turned my head to stare out the window until we made it to Devil Springs.

12

COAL

When the clubhouse came into view, I could see a small crowd of people in the field where Shaker was going to land.

As soon as we touched down, Tatum and Luke were at the door, jerking it open and climbing inside. Tatum grabbed the microphone attached to my dad's headset and pulled it toward her as she leaned down to speak. "There's a Jane Doe at a hospital in Pinebrook matching Aspen's description. I've already filed a flight plan and made arrangements for you to land at the closest airport."

"Why would she be listed as a Jane Doe?" I asked and suddenly wished I hadn't. There were only a few possible answers, and none of them were good.

"Because they haven't been able to make a positive identification," Tatum said cryptically.

"Why?" I demanded. "What's wrong with her?"

Tatum grimaced. "The woman was picked up by an ambulance with a head injury and a gunshot wound.

She lost consciousness en route and is currently in a medically induced coma."

"She was shot?" I shouted. "Where? Do they think she's going to live? What else do you know?"

Tatum held her hands up and gave me a sympathetic look. "We don't know for sure that it's Aspen. Until we can confirm that it is, the information they were willing to share was limited. They would only tell me that she had a gunshot wound and two skull fractures, but they assured me she was stable."

The rest of the group continued to talk, but I completely zoned out. I couldn't stop the images of Aspen lying in a hospital bed, bloodied and bruised, from flooding my mind. What had she been through? What if she never woke up? What if she didn't make it? What if she did and didn't remember me or was a completely different person? None of those possibilities were acceptable.

I felt a hand on my shoulder and turned to see my uncle watching me with worry-filled eyes. "I'm pretty sure I know what's going through your mind right now. Because the same things are going through mine. And the truth is, we won't know the answers to those questions for a while. But one thing we do know is that Aspen is strong and resilient. If this is her, she'll fight like hell to survive."

He was right. If anyone could pull through, it was Aspen. I felt so torn. I wanted it to be her, because that would mean we found her, but at the same time, I didn't want it to be her, because I didn't want her to have such severe injuries.

"Do you think it's her?" I asked. Deep down, I felt

like it was, and I wondered if he felt the same. Not knowing was killing me.

"Yeah, I do," he admitted. "But we'll know for sure soon enough."

I closed my eyes and leaned back against the headrest for the remainder of the flight. Thankfully, no one disturbed me. I needed whatever time we had left to pull myself together. Aspen needed me, and I wanted to be the best I could for her.

The ride from the airport to the hospital was a blur. It could have been fifteen minutes, or it could have been an hour. I had no clue. Exhaustion from my own ordeal was trying to take over, but I refused to let myself rest until I knew where Aspen was.

I jolted when Dad nudged me with his elbow. "We're here."

We filed out of the car and into the hospital as a unit. When the woman at the front desk looked up, her eyes widened at the sight of us.

"Can I help you?" she asked cautiously.

"Luke Johnson, FBI," my uncle said and presented his badge to her. "I need to speak to the person caring for the Jane Doe you have in ICU."

"Yes, sir," she said and reached for the phone. "They're expecting you. If you'd like to take a seat, I'll let them know you're here."

No one sat. We stayed right where we were and waited for the nurse.

A woman appeared moments later and introduced herself as the director of the intensive care unit. "Follow me, and I'll take you upstairs to a private waiting room. Per hospital policy, I can only allow one law enforcement officer and one family member to go into the room to identify her. If a positive ID is made, then we'll allow family to visit."

"I'm the agent in charge of the missing woman's case, and this is her fiancé," my uncle explained and gestured to me. "We'll be the ones identifying her."

We left the rest of the group in the designated waiting room and followed the woman down the hall.

My heart was pounding so hard in my chest I could hear it in my ears, and it seemed to get louder with each step I took.

When we reached the room, I was surprised to see a security guard outside of her room. Without thought, I extended my hand to him. "Thank you for watching over her."

He shook my hand and nodded in acknowledgment.

"Here she is," the director said and slowly pushed the door open.

I gasped at the sight of her and immediately went to her side.

"It's her," I heard my uncle say. "Her name is Aspen White."

I leaned over the bed and carefully placed my hands on her pale cheeks. "I love you so much," I told her and kissed her forehead. "I'm sorry I wasn't there to protect you. But I'm here now, and I'm not going anywhere." Tears were streaming down my face, and I didn't give the first fuck who saw them. I'd almost lost the love of my life, and I was beyond relieved to have her in front of me, regardless of what shape she was in.

"You need to sit down before you fall over," Luke instructed as he pushed a chair toward me.

"How is she?" I asked without taking my eyes off of Aspen.

"The doctor is going to come in and talk to us about her injuries," Luke explained.

I lowered myself into the chair and exhaled slowly. "This is such a strange feeling. I'm happy we found her, but seeing her like this is awful."

"I know exactly what you mean. I think I wanted it to be her just as much as I didn't."

A knock on the door had us both turning to see a man dressed in scrubs and a white lab coat entering the room.

"Hello, I'm Dr. Cornell. I'm one of the physicians taking care of Ms. Doe."

"Ms. White," I corrected. "Her name is Aspen White."

"Actually, given the circumstances, I think we should leave her as Jane Doe for the time being," Luke suggested. "Will that be a problem?"

"No, not at all."

"What's wrong with her?" I asked bluntly.

"She was brought in last night with a gunshot wound to her chest and a head injury. From what I understand, someone saw her walking along the highway and called an ambulance. She lost consciousness shortly after she was picked up and didn't regain it before she was taken to surgery to remove the bullet and repair the damages it caused. The bullet hit her lung and caused it to collapse, which is why she has a chest tube. After surgery, she was placed in a medically induced coma to allow her brain to heal. She has two skull fractures, both along the back of her head. Whatever trauma caused those also caused her brain to swell. So far, she doesn't need surgical intervention, but we are monitoring her closely for any changes. Overall, considering her injuries, she's doing well, but she's not out of the woods yet by any means."

"When will she wake up?"

"I wish I could give you a solid answer, but I don't have one. We'll keep her sedated for a few more days. After that, it's up to her. She could wake up within a couple of hours, or it could be days, possibly longer."

So, there was a possibility she would never wake up. That's what he was saying without coming right out and saying it.

"Do you have any other questions?" he asked.

I shook my head and turned to Luke.

"Not at this time," he answered.

"If you think of any, please let us know."

Once he was gone, the rest of the group piled into the room. Thankfully, it was large enough to accommodate us comfortably.

"All right, what's the plan?" Tatum asked, getting right down to business.

"Coal is obviously going to stay here with Aspen, but you and I need to get back to Devil Springs," Luke started.

"I'm staying here," my dad announced. "She needs protection. They both do, and I'm not leaving that in the hands of hospital security."

Luke grinned. "I was hoping you'd say that."

"I'm sure Annabelle and Kathleen have made it to Devil Springs by now. When Shaker drops you and Tatum off, he can pick them up and bring them here. Dash, I want you with them at all times."

"Can someone get me a change of clothes and

whatever else I might need for the next few days?" I asked.

"I can take care of that," Dash volunteered.

"Ask Game. He knows where all of my shit is. Oh, and can you get a burner phone from Copper? I don't know what happened to mine."

"Your phone was found in your driveway," Luke shared. "It should be at the clubhouse, but I think you should use a burner for now and leave your phone where it is. Just in case someone is tracking it."

The thought of someone tracking my phone hadn't even occurred to me. "I guess that's why they pay you the big bucks."

He grinned. "Might be."

Luke walked over to the bed and dropped a kiss on top of Aspen's head before whispering something I couldn't hear. Then he turned to me and ruffled my hair. "You take care of our girl, and I'll take care of everything else."

"I'll do my best," I said and rose to my feet to hug him.

Once everyone was gone, my dad turned to me with a concerned look on his face. "Let me see your wrists."

"What? Why?" I asked, fighting the urge to hide my hands behind my back.

"Because you're hurt. You've done a damn good job of hiding it, but you've barely moved your hands since we found you. Plus, I've seen you cradling your wrists when you thought no one was looking. Now that everyone's gone, let me see."

"Fine, but I'm not leaving her no matter how bad they look," I insisted.

"You won't have to. We'll get someone to come to the room if need be."

"Okay," I sighed and started to roll up my sleeves but stopped when I realized my shirt was stuck to my raw skin in several places.

Before I could open my mouth to explain, Dad pressed the call light and asked for a nurse to come to the room.

"You're aware of our special situation?" Dad asked when she entered the room.

"Yes, sir," she confirmed.

"In relation to this case, my son was injured. He needs some medical attention, but he's not going to leave her side to get it. Is there any way we could have someone come up to the room to see him?"

"That depends. What kind of injury are we talking about?"

I peeled back a part of my shirt that wasn't adhered to my skin and showed her as much as I could.

Her eyes widened at the sight. The skin around my wrists was raw and bloody, and my hands and fingers were significantly swollen.

"Let me grab a few things, and I'll see what I can do."

She returned with a load of supplies and closed the door behind her. She took her time, but when all was said and done, she'd separated my shirt from my skin, cleaned my wounds, and wrapped my wrists with gauze. Then, she handed me a bag of ice for the swelling.

"You need to keep a close eye on the wounds for any sign of infection. If you think it is getting infected, you need to see a doctor as soon as possible so they can put you on antibiotics," she explained.

"I'll be sure to stay on top of that," Dad replied. "Thank you for your help."

"Yes, thank you," I added.

"Is there anything else I can do for you?"

"Actually, yes, there is. He'll be staying with her until she's discharged. Do you guys have a cot or fold-out bed for overnight visitors?"

"We sure do," she smiled. "I'll have someone from housekeeping bring one up for you. For safety reasons, we can only allow one per room, but we can swap that chair out for a recliner if both of you will be staying the night."

"Yes, we'll both be here. Thank you."

"Great. I'll go call for your bed now."

"What about my moms?" I asked after she left the room.

"Dash is going to stay with them at the hotel across the street after they've had a chance to see you and Aspen."

I glanced at the clock on the wall. "I didn't realize how late it was. They probably should have waited until tomorrow to come."

Dad laughed. "Are you serious? There's no way. The only reason they waited this long is because they didn't have a choice. But I can guarantee if Shaker wasn't flying them, they'd be driving. You're their son, and they've been worried sick. They aren't going to feel any better until they've seen you."

* * *

DAYS PASSED, BUT NOTHING MUCH HAD CHANGED. They'd stopped the medicine keeping Aspen in a coma, but she hadn't woken up or shown any signs indicating she was close to waking up.

They told us she was stable and was healing well. Her chest tube was removed after her lung reinflated, but she was still on oxygen, which they assured us was normal. They also said she no longer needed to be in intensive care, but agreed to let her stay in the unit as long as they had the availability since it was a closed unit and more secure than the regular patient rooms.

Both of my moms were still in town and stayed at the hospital during the day, while my dad never left my side.

Luke called frequently to check on Aspen, but I was starting to dread his calls. I hated having to tell him nothing had changed. I also hated hearing him tell me they hadn't made any progress in Aspen's case. They had named Pamela as the primary suspect, but no one, not even me, had been able to say with one hundred percent certainty that she was involved. For all anyone knew, we could be focusing on Pamela while the real culprit was long gone.

"You seem pretty down today," Mom observed. "What's on your mind?"

I'd kept most of my thoughts and speculations to myself, but no one had directly asked me until that moment. So, I opened my mouth and spewed every thought, theory, and wonder that had crossed my mind since Aspen and I were found.

"It was her," a familiar yet raspy voice said. It was the voice I'd longed to hear and feared I never would again.

"Aspen!" I gasped and almost tripped over my feet to

get to her. She slowly opened her eyes and immediately scrunched her face.

"What's wrong? Are you in pain?"

"Yeah," she said weakly and closed her eyes. "My head really hurts."

"I'll get the nurse," Mom said and stepped out of the room.

Once again, I felt torn. I didn't want her to be in pain, but I also didn't want the pain medicine to knock her out when I'd just gotten her back.

"I'm so happy you're awake," I admitted. "You're going to be okay. Everything's going to be okay."

She cracked her eyes open and glanced around the room. "I'm in the hospital." It sounded more like a statement than a question, but I still nodded in response. "How long have I been here?"

"Four days. You said it was Pamela. Do you remember what happened?"

"She was waiting for me after work. She got in the passenger seat, pointed a gun at me, and told me to drive. We were on the highway for a long time, but I'm not sure where I took her."

Before I could ask her any other questions, her nurse entered the room and started examining her. She asked her a series of questions, shined a light in her eyes, and gave her something for her pain.

"What happened to me?" Aspen asked as soon as the nurse left the room.

"I'm not entirely sure. Someone saw you on the side of the road and called an ambulance. You were brought to the hospital with a head injury, and you'd been shot in the chest," I explained carefully, unsure of how she would react.

"Well, that explains why it hurts like a motherfucker when I breathe," she said flatly.

Her reaction, or lack thereof, wasn't what I expected. "You sure you're okay?"

"Yeah, I think so," she confirmed and exhaled slowly. "I'm just trying to decide if I'm more shocked by the fact that she actually shot me or that I can't remember it."

"Trust me, not remembering it is a good thing," I said, speaking from my own experience. I vividly recalled everything about being shot and wholeheartedly wished I didn't.

"Yeah, you're probably right," she said as her eyes started to droop. Suddenly, they popped open. "Where's Luke? Does he know what happened?"

"He does. He's back in Devil Springs trying to find Pamela. Do you want me to call him?"

"Yes, please."

I dialed his number and handed my phone to her. "Coal, please tell me you have good news," I heard him say.

"He has good news," Aspen said with a small smile.

"Aspen," he breathed. "I'm so happy to hear your voice. How are you feeling?"

"I've had better days."

They continued to talk for several minutes before she held the phone out to me. "He wants to talk to you."

"Get as much information from her as you can, but don't press her too hard. I'm going to work on making arrangements to have her moved back to Devil Springs now that she's awake, but we don't need any setbacks between now and then."

"Understood."

I resumed my position at Aspen's side and took her hand in mine. It wasn't long before her pain medicine kicked in, and she fell asleep. And for the first time since we were both taken, I fell into a deep, restful sleep right beside her.

13

PHOENIX

When my phone rang with a number I didn't recognize, I stepped out of Aspen's room to answer it. Coal was sound asleep for the first time in days, and I didn't want to risk waking him. The boy had been running on fumes and needed any rest he could get.

"Phoenix Black," I answered.

"Hey, Phoenix. This is Jimmy Sullivan. I'm the one who found your son in the woods."

"Yes, of course. What can I do for you, Jimmy?"

"Well, I'm not sure, to be honest. I had a couple of agents come to my door today asking about a missing hiker. I can't put my finger on it, but something about them didn't sit right with me."

"I see. And you think this has something to do with my son?" I guessed.

"I didn't at first, but the description they gave matched your son, even the clothes he was wearing." He cleared his throat and lowered his voice. "Your son's business ain't my business, but we both know that boy didn't get lost while camping with his friends. That was obvious by the state he was in when we crossed paths. If I had to take a guess, I'd say whoever he got away from is trying to figure out where he went."

"I see. May I ask what you told the agents?"

"I told them I hadn't seen anybody on my property in years and left it at that."

"You think they believed you?"

"They seemed to. They apologized for bothering me and left a card with a phone number to call if I saw anyone matching the description they gave me."

"Really? Would you mind sharing that contact information with me?"

"Sure thing. I'll send a picture of it to your phone right now."

"Thanks, man. I can't get into the details, but your instincts were spot on. And I have a feeling this contact information is going to be extremely helpful to me."

"I learned a long time ago to trust my feelings. Glad I could help."

"Before you go, can you tell me what the agents looked like?"

"The female was tall and thin. Some might say she was a looker, but she had an evilness in her eyes that I found off-putting. She had shoulder-length blonde hair and wore way too much makeup for my taste. The male was about the same height as her. He had short, dark hair. Average build. He was quite plain looking compared to her. It was pretty obvious she was the one running the show."

"Got it. I really appreciate you calling. Can I reach you at this number if any questions come up?"

"You sure can," he confirmed. "I don't have

reception out at the cabin, but if you leave a message, I'll call you back as soon as I get it."

"Great. Thanks again, Jimmy."

"No problem," he said and ended the call.

With my phone still in my hand, I flipped to my messages and looked at the picture Jimmy sent. It was a plain, white business card with the name John Smith and a phone number printed on the front. There was nothing on the card to indicate it belonged to any kind of law enforcement officer, which is likely why Jimmy thought it was suspicious.

I forwarded the message to Luke before placing a call to him.

"Phoenix, everything okay?" he answered.

"Yeah, everything's fine. I just got a call from the man who found Coal in the woods," I started and filled him in on my conversation with Jimmy.

"I don't recognize the name or number, but it's likely a fake name and a phone number to a throw-away phone. Regardless, I'll check into it."

"Do you think it was her?"

"It could be. It certainly sounds like her. We could send him a picture of her and ask," he suggested.

"Send me one, and I'll forward it to him."

"Sent."

"Got it. I'll let you know what he says."

Once again, I forwarded a message and placed a call.

"Hey, Jimmy, it's Phoenix Black."

"Well, hello, Phoenix. I didn't expect to hear from you so soon."

"I didn't expect to be calling so soon. Listen, I just sent a picture to your phone. I was wondering if the woman in the picture is the woman who came to your door."

"Let me have a look," he said. "Oh yes, that's definitely her."

"You're sure?"

"One hundred percent," he confirmed.

"Did you happen to see what kind of car they were driving?"

"Sure did. It was a black sedan. Not sure if it was a Honda or a Toyota, but I did get the license plate number."

"Appreciate it, man. I'm sure you're more than capable of handling yourself, but it's worth mentioning that she's dangerous. She's not affiliated with any kind of law enforcement."

"I knew something wasn't right with her. I'll keep my eyes and ears open and let you know if I see her again."

"Thanks, Jimmy."

Then, I called Luke back to let him know Jimmy had identified Pamela as the woman impersonating a federal agent and gave him the description of their vehicle as well as the tag number.

"We're going to owe Jimmy another dinner after all this," Luke said.

"And then some," I agreed. Because finally, we had something to go on.

14

ASPEN

Three days had passed since I'd woken up in a hospital room with Coal at my side. I was still in a good bit of pain and couldn't do much for myself, but each day seemed to be a little better than the one before. Even though I thought I was progressing slower than I should be, the nurses and doctors assured me that I was doing great, and some even said I was doing better than expected. I assumed they said that to all the patients to keep them from getting discouraged, so I was completely caught off guard when the doctor came in and told me I was being discharged.

"What?" I asked in surprise. "Like right now?"

He laughed. "Not right this second, but sometime today. It'll take a few hours to get everything in order."

"Are you sure I'm ready to go home?"

"Yes, you are. Keep in mind that being discharged from the hospital doesn't mean you're healed and can resume your normal activities. It just means you don't require this level of care anymore. Your nurse will go over your instructions and restrictions with you before you leave. I assume you have someone who will be around to help you for the first few days," he said and looked pointedly at Coal.

"Yes, she does," Coal answered.

"Great. I'll get started on your discharge orders now," he said and left the room.

"I can't believe they're letting me go home. I thought for sure I'd be here for a few more days."

"I did, too," he admitted. "But I'm not complaining. I think we'll both be more comfortable at home."

"When you say home, do you mean my house or yours?" I asked. I didn't care where we were, as long as we were together.

"Actually, I meant the clubhouse. With Pamela still out there, it's the safest place for us."

I nodded in understanding, even though I wasn't thrilled with his answer.

"What's wrong?"

"I don't want to hide from her forever." I couldn't explain it, but even though she'd attacked me and tried to kill me, I wasn't scared of her. Maybe because I wasn't expecting it before, but now I knew to be more alert.

"You aren't hiding from her. You're healing. If she hasn't been found by the time you're completely healed, we'll go home. But for now, the clubhouse is secure, and there will always be someone around to help you if you need it."

"I know. I'm just frustrated with the whole situation. I thought Pamela was finally out of my life when she went to prison years ago. Yet here she is again, trying to ruin my life. I don't know why she hates me so much, and frankly, I don't care. I just want to be rid of her for good."

"We're doing everything we can to make that happen for you," he promised.

"Thank you," I said and felt tears begin to fill my eyes. "For finding me, taking care of me, and staying by my side through all of this."

He gently cupped my cheek with his large hand. "I love you, Aspen. By your side is where I'll always be."

"I love you, too," I said softly. "More than I ever knew was possible."

"Good, because you're stuck with me."

"Promise?"

"With my whole heart."

* * *

SEVERAL HOURS LATER, WE WERE LOADED INTO A LARGE SUV and headed back to Devil Springs with Phoenix behind the wheel.

I was dressed in the new pajamas Annabelle and Kathleen bought for me since I didn't have any other clothes to wear. I had a pillow behind my head and was wrapped in a blanket with Coal snuggled beside me. It was the most comfortable I'd been since the attack.

I was staring out the window listening to the others talk when we passed a car that looked a lot like mine, which prompted me to ask. "Where's my car?"

"What?" Coal asked.

"My car. Where is it?"

"We're assuming Pamela drove away in it after she shot you, but we haven't been able to locate it yet," Phoenix told me.

Well, that was just fucking great. Yet another problem I'd have to deal with thanks to Pamela. At least I had time to get it sorted since I wasn't allowed to drive for a few more weeks.

"Has it been reported stolen?" I asked, knowing I would need to do that in order to file an insurance claim so I could get a replacement.

"I'm pretty sure Luke was taking care of that for you. I'll mention it the next time I talk to him. But don't worry about it too much. If it isn't sorted by the time you're cleared to drive, you can use one of the club's loaner cars."

"It's pretty impressive how you guys seem to have a solution to every problem."

"They're like badass Boy Scouts," Annabelle said. "Always prepared."

"Speaking of being prepared, if you'll make a list of the stuff you'll need from your house for the next few weeks, we'll have someone go over and get it."

I leaned over and whispered to Coal, "Who are they going to send? I'm not sure I'm comfortable with your club brothers digging through my underwear drawer."

He chuckled. "Then don't put bras and panties on the list. We can ask one of the girls to run to the store and pick up some new ones for you."

"Are you sure they won't mind? I don't want to be any more trouble than I already am."

"Aspen, it's no trouble. You're family. This is what we do," Coal explained.

"Technically, I'm not family, but I like your answer."

"Technically, you are," he countered.

"How so?"

He shifted slightly. "I was waiting for the right time

to tell you, and I'm not sure this is it, but I claimed you as my Old Lady right after we found you." I opened my mouth to speak, but he held up his hand to stop me. "I was planning on doing it anyway, but after almost losing you, I wasn't willing to let another second go by without you being officially mine. We can talk about it when we have more privacy if you're not okay with it."

I couldn't keep the smile from spreading across my face. "No need. I'm more than okay with it."

"Thank fuck," he breathed and pressed his lips to mine.

He broke the kiss far too soon for my liking and gave me a knowing look. "When you're better," he promised.

I made a mental note to see what my discharge instructions said about sex. I didn't remember them mentioning it and hadn't thought to ask.

"Do you think sex falls under vigorous activity?" I whispered.

"Yes, I do," he grinned. "So you'll have to contain yourself for the next two weeks."

"Two weeks?" I blurted, louder than I intended.

"Maybe it was three," he teased.

"I know it wasn't three," I said with certainty.

"We'll check the papers when we get home."

"When will that be?" I asked and yawned. The pain pill I'd taken before we left the hospital had kicked in, and I could feel myself getting drowsy. I hated that they made me so sleepy, but I was also grateful for the relief they provided.

"We've got at least another hour to go. Go ahead and close your eyes. I'll wake you when we get there."

* * *

He didn't wake me when we arrived. Instead, I woke up in his bed at the clubhouse. Coal was beside me with his arm draped across my abdomen, resting heavily on my very full bladder.

I knew he was exhausted, so I tried to get out of bed without disturbing him. However, the moment I moved his arm, he was wide awake. "You okay?"

"I'm fine. I just need to pee."

He hopped out of bed like he hadn't just woken up from a deep sleep and helped me to my feet before escorting me to the bathroom. Despite the progress I'd made, I was still unsteady on my feet and needed help to move around.

Once I was back in bed, he sat down beside me. "How are you feeling?"

"I'm a little sore, but otherwise okay for the moment. What time is it?"

He picked up his phone from the nightstand and checked the time. "A little after six. Are you hungry?"

"Not really, but I probably should try to eat something. I'm not supposed to take any of the medicines they gave me on an empty stomach."

He typed out a message on his phone and climbed back into the bed beside me.

"Um, what are you doing? I thought you were going to get food."

"Wait for it," he grinned.

Not even five minutes later, someone knocked on the door.

"Come in," he called.

The door opened, and Kathleen walked in, carrying a large tray of food. "I heard someone was hungry."

"Oh, you didn't have to do that," I smiled. "But thank you, it smells wonderful."

"I thought you should have a nice home-cooked meal after suffering through days of hospital food."

"So it wasn't just me?" I asked, causing them both to laugh.

"No, it wasn't. The food really was awful," Coal agreed.

I placed a bite of food in my mouth and moaned at the taste. "This is delicious."

"I'm glad you like it. Eat up. There's plenty more where that came from."

"Seriously, this is hands down the best lasagna I've ever had."

"Well, if I didn't already think she was perfect for you, I certainly do now," Kathleen said.

I wasn't sure what she meant, so I looked to Coal for clarification.

"This is my favorite meal. She used to make it for me once a week until I moved to Devil Springs. Now, she makes it every time I go home for a visit."

"I have a feeling we'll be visiting often," I said and continued to devour my meal. Surprisingly, I was able to finish everything on my plate, including my drink, despite not feeling hungry.

"Are you sure you got enough? I'll be happy to make you another plate," Kathleen offered.

"Thank you, but I'm good. I probably overdid it as it is. I never eat that much in one sitting, but I couldn't seem to help myself."

"Your body was probably starving for actual sustenance. Who can survive off of watered-down broth and sugar-free Jell-O?"

I scrunched my face in disgust. "If I never see green Jell-O again, it'll still be too soon."

"At least you were the patient. The food they had for the visitors was much worse," Coal pointed out.

"You should've said something. I would've gladly shared my Jell-O with you."

"That sounds like a threat," he teased.

"It might be."

"Well, if you two are sure you don't want anything else, I'll get out of your hair."

"Thanks, Mom. I think we're good for now."

"Be sure to let me know if that changes," she said and headed for the door. "Oh, I almost forgot. Luke came by to see you earlier, but he didn't want to wake you. He asked me to call him if you felt like having visitors once you were awake."

"Yes, please. Luke is always welcome, even if I am sleeping."

She smiled sweetly. "I'll let him know."

When Luke arrived, he walked right over to the bed and wrapped me up in a hug. "You look so much better than the last time I saw you," he said and tightened his arms around me, causing a small groan to escape me.

"Shit, I'm sorry," he said and released his hold on me. "Did I hurt you?"

"No, I just ate, and I'm really, really full. Blame your sister."

He laughed. "I should've known. She's all about the comfort food when a loved one is sick or injured."

"You'll hear no complaints from me."

He reached out and smoothed his hand over my hair. "I'm so glad you're home and doing better. You had me worried for a minute there."

"I still have a way to go, but I'm glad to be home, too."

He pulled up a chair and took a seat, clasping his hands in his lap. "There are a few things we need to discuss," he said carefully.

"By 'things,' do you mean Pamela?"

"Yes. I'm not sure how much you know, so I thought I'd start at the beginning to make sure I don't miss anything."

"That sounds good to me. I really don't know much of anything other than she made me drive her out to the middle of nowhere and tried to kill me."

"Back in December, she disappeared after two bodies were found on her property. One was an associate of hers, and one was a private investigator who had been hired by her late husband's son. Since both died in the same manner as her husband, his death investigation has been reopened."

"You obviously think she killed them, but do you know why?" I asked.

"The working theory is she killed her husband for his money. He changed his will right before his death, leaving everything he had to her, which was several million dollars. His son immediately contested the will and hired a private investigator. We think the PI found something to prove the will wasn't valid, so she killed him to keep him quiet. As for her associate, we haven't been able to pinpoint a reason, but we're still sifting through all the evidence. Unfortunately, with cases of this magnitude, it can take months before we have all the answers."

"Months?" I asked in disbelief.

"Months before we have all the answers. That

doesn't mean it will be months before we locate Pamela. As of right now, we have more than enough to arrest her once we've found her," he clarified.

"How close are you to finding her? Do you have any idea where she is?"

"She was recently spotted in the area where Coal was found."

"How do you know it was her?"

"She was posing as a federal agent. A witness reported it and positively identified her from a picture. She did have a man with her, but we haven't been able to identify him yet."

I wasn't sure if it was because of my head injury, but I was having a hard time connecting the dots. "What does any of this have to do with me and Coal?"

Luke pinched the bridge of his nose and sighed. "As a result of her being suspected of murdering her husband and the will being contested, all of her assets have been frozen. In other words, she needs money."

I couldn't help but laugh. "And what made her think she'd be able to get any money from me?"

"The five-million-dollar life insurance policy she has on you."

"The what?" I almost shouted.

"She has a life insurance policy on you worth five million dollars," he repeated.

"That still doesn't make any sense. She left me for dead on a dirt road in the middle of nowhere. There's no telling how long it would've taken someone to find me."

Luke suddenly sat forward in his seat. "How do you know you were on a dirt road? Did you remember something?"

I shook my head. "No, not really. I get little flashes of things here and there. Me walking on an unpaved road in the dark. Then, me walking on a paved road. I remember my head feeling like it was going to explode. And I remember being cold. At least, I think they're memories. They could just as easily be something I made up."

I'd tried numerous times to remember anything about that night, but each time left me frustrated and made my head hurt.

"Hold on a minute," Coal said. "Let's say she did try to kill Aspen for the insurance money. How was she going to get it and stay under the radar?"

Luke shrugged. "We haven't figured that part out yet, but Pamela's a clever woman. I have no doubt she had a plan in place."

"I suppose it doesn't really matter anymore, since I'm clearly not dead," I pointed out.

"About that," Luke started but seemed hesitant to continue. "I have an idea that might speed things along and put an end to this whole ordeal if we can pull it off, but I don't think you're going to like it."

"It doesn't matter if I like it if it gets rid of Pamela once and for all. Let's hear it."

"As far as we know, she doesn't know you're alive. I think we should fake your death and let her claim the insurance money. We should be able to pick her up when she goes to collect it."

"You think that will work?"

"I think there's a good chance it will, as long as I can get the insurance company to work with us. I wanted to talk to you first before I mentioned it to anyone else. If you agree, you'll have to stay hidden until we catch her."

"Oh," I said, suddenly understanding why he thought I wouldn't like his plan. "For how long?"

"Life insurance policies take anywhere from fourteen to thirty days to pay out. Then, we'd have to wait for her to access the money."

"I'd be gone for a month? Where would I go? And what about my job?" I asked, rattling off questions in quick succession.

"Slow down and take a breath," Luke instructed. "You don't have to do this. You can say no, and we'll find another way. If you agree, you'll be moved to a safe house with federal agents and other trained staff, so you won't be alone. I can't say for sure how long you'd be there, but I promise I'll move things along as fast as I can. As for your job, you can't go back to work for a few more weeks anyway, but I'll make sure your job is waiting for you if this happens to take longer than expected."

"What about Coal? Will I be able to see him?" I asked.

Luke shook his head. "No, we can't risk blowing our cover if she somehow spots him frequenting a new location. If she is watching him, Coal needs to be seen around town looking like his girlfriend just died."

"Do I have to decide right now?"

"Of course not. Take some time to talk about it and think it over, and I'll check in with you tomorrow." With that, he placed a kiss on my forehead, said goodbye to Coal, and left the room.

Before I had a chance to ask what he thought, Coal volunteered his opinion. "I think you should do it."

"Yeah, I kind of do too. But I don't want to be gone for a month."

"I know it seems like a long time, but think about it this way. Is a month of your time worth being rid of Pamela forever?"

"Yes, but there's no guarantee this will work. Then what? Will I be able to resume my normal life, or will I need to stay dead indefinitely?"

"That's something you need to ask Luke," Coal said and got up to get a pen and some paper. "Keep talking. I'll make a list of questions to ask him tomorrow."

We spent the rest of the evening discussing the pros and cons as well as various possible scenarios and outcomes, resulting in a lengthy list of questions for Luke. But I knew I was going to agree to his plan, regardless of the answers he gave. Because Pamela was an evil person who had put me and the man I loved in danger. It would be selfish of me not to do everything I could to help put her behind bars for good.

15

ASPEN

It had been a little over three weeks since I died. And it felt like I was slowly losing my mind. I was bored and restless and was very much ready to go home. And I missed Coal so much it physically hurt sometimes.

On top of that, not knowing what was going on was maddening. I wasn't given any updates unless I specifically asked, and even those were few and far between.

The first update was about my "death." They used the truth as the first part of the story—I was found walking along the highway with a head injury and a gunshot wound. Then, after being discharged from the hospital, I died at home from a suspected blood clot. The story was featured on several news channels and websites in the surrounding areas, asking anyone with information to come forward.

It didn't take long for Pamela to see the story and contact the insurance company.

The next update came two weeks later when the insurance money was paid out.

Four days later, they were still waiting on Pamela to access the money. And with each day that passed, I grew more and more anxious. What was she waiting for?

The sound of someone knocking on my door made my heart jump, just like it did every single time someone knocked since I'd been there. I'd grown to hate the sound as much as I anticipated it.

I opened the door, hoping it would be Tatum or Josie telling me they'd caught her and I could go home. But like all the times before, I was once again disappointed.

"Lunch is ready," Josie said cheerfully.

"Thanks, but I'm not hungry," I said solemnly.

"That's okay. You don't have to eat anything. But will you join me anyway?"

I wanted to say no and continue sulking in my room, but I couldn't bring myself to refuse her request. She'd been so kind to me and really made an effort to keep my spirits up during my stay. I had to admit, having familiar faces around had made my stay more bearable. I couldn't imagine what it would have been like if I'd been placed in a house with complete strangers.

"You seem pretty down today," she observed. "Do you want to talk about it?"

"I'm just frustrated. I don't understand what is taking so long. The money is sitting there waiting for her. Why isn't she going to get it?"

"You can't just walk into a bank and withdraw five million dollars. A transaction of that magnitude takes time to prepare," she explained.

"It's been four days. It feels like I'm never going to get out of here."

"I know," she said. And she did. She'd told me all

about the time she spent hidden away in the safe house. "But it shouldn't be too much longer."

"I hope you're right."

"Do you want to help me with some book reviews for the blog? It might take your mind off things and help the time pass a little faster."

"I can try, but I've been having a hard time concentrating for more than a few minutes at a time. I'm not sure if it's related to my head injury or because I'm worried about what's happening out there while I'm stuck in here."

"It's probably a little bit of both. If you feel up to it, you're welcome to do what you can. If not, that's okay too. But I'm not going to let you stay closed up in your room all day."

I spent the next few hours typing up book reviews and blog posts for her. She claimed she didn't like typing and preferred to handwrite her reviews, but I had a feeling she was only doing that so I would have something to do. And for that, I was grateful, because it did make the time go by faster.

"Do you want to help me make dinner?" she asked when we'd finished with her reviews.

"Sure. What are you making?"

"I found a vodka pasta recipe online that's supposed to be really good. Does that sound okay to you?"

Nothing sounded appealing to me. My stomach had been in knots since I arrived at the safe house, and it was a daily struggle to eat. Since there wasn't anything she could do to change that, I nodded and lied. "Sounds great."

The dish was relatively easy to make and made the house smell wonderful. I even managed to have a few bites and a piece of garlic bread before I felt like I was going to be sick. Josie, however, had no problem finishing everything on her plate.

I glanced at the time on the stove. "Where's Tatum? Shouldn't she have been home by now?"

"She called and said she was going to be late because she had a meeting to go to."

After we cleaned up and put the leftovers away, Josie asked if I wanted to watch a movie with her, but I declined her offer. I appreciated her keeping me occupied for the majority of the day, but I was ready to be alone in my room where I didn't feel compelled to put on a brave face.

After a quick shower, I climbed into bed and willed myself not to cry. But I couldn't help myself. I burst into tears and cried myself to sleep.

16

LUKE

After days of waiting and watching for Pamela to show up at the bank, I finally spotted her. Her hair was shorter and darker than it usually was, and she tried to disguise herself with a large hat and sunglasses, but I recognized her instantly.

I had already alerted my team and was on my way across the street to the bank when my phone vibrated with a message from the bank manager telling me what I already knew. Pamela was in the building.

Picking up my pace, I entered the bank through the back door and went to the office we'd previously designated to use for Pamela's transaction.

Pamela entered the room first, followed by the manager, who closed the door behind them. I waited until they were both seated to step out from the shadows and make my presence known.

"Pamela Perry, you're under arrest," I started but was interrupted by Pamela's laughter.

"Oh, Luke, did you really think I wouldn't be prepared for this?" she asked and slowly stood up.

Then, she turned to me and ripped her shirt open to reveal a bomb strapped to her chest. She smirked. "I suggest you choose your next move very carefully."

"The only way you're leaving this building is in handcuffs or a body bag. The choice is yours," I said calmly with my gun trained on her.

I could hear a flurry of activity outside of the office, but I didn't dare take my eyes off of her to turn and see what was happening on the other side of the glass wall behind me. Assuming it was members from my team and the bank's security clearing the building, I tried to buy them some time by keeping her talking.

I nodded toward the bank manager. "This doesn't have anything to do with him. Why don't you let him leave while we sort this out," I suggested.

"And give up an innocent hostage I could otherwise use to my advantage?" she shook her head. "Clearly, I'm not as dumb as you think I am."

"Oh, I've never thought you were dumb. But I do think you're desperate."

Her face contorted with anger, and she opened her mouth to respond, but managed to get control of herself before she did. Which was unfortunate, because I was hoping to upset her enough that she'd slip up and give me an opportunity to apprehend her without blowing us all to smithereens.

Bombs weren't my specialty, so I didn't know anything about the one she was wearing. There appeared to be a button to push to activate it, but it was anyone's guess as to how strong it was.

When the phone in the office rang, the manager looked at me with wide, fear-filled eyes.

"Answer it," I said at the same time Pamela said, "Don't answer it."

"They'll keep calling until someone picks up. You have to talk to them to negotiate."

"I'm not negotiating," she said and pointed to the manager. "You are going to get my money." Then, she turned to me. "And you are going to call off your team. Then, you and I are going to walk out of here, get in my car, and drive away. I have no problem killing you or anyone else if they try to follow us or stop us."

She emphasized her point by producing a gun from her pocket and shooting the phone when it started to ring again. The bank manager screamed and ducked under his desk as the phone exploded into pieces.

"Was it really necessary to shoot the phone?" I asked, letting those listening to the microphone hidden under my shirt know what was transpiring in the office since I didn't know how much they could see.

"None of this would have been necessary if you would've minded your own business. But you can't seem to help yourself when it comes to me, can you?"

"I'm doing my job, Pamela. If you don't want me to get involved, stop breaking the law."

"I'll be sure to get right on that. As soon as I get my money." She tapped on the desk with the barrel of her gun. "That means you. Get moving."

"Yes, ma'am," he said shakily and crawled out from under his desk with his hands raised in front of him. "I need to go to the vault to get it."

"We'll join you. Lead the way," Pamela instructed. She didn't seem the slightest bit concerned that I still had my gun trained on her as we moved to the vault.

She likely knew I wouldn't risk shooting her and setting off the bomb, but her confidence irritated me.

While we were waiting, she pointed to a nearby phone and told me to call off my team.

"You do realize it's not just my team. By now, the local police have been alerted and are on scene."

"Then I suggest your buddies make sure they know to stand down."

I picked up the phone and called Dave, quickly relaying Pamela's plan. He, of course, had been listening and was well aware of what was going on.

"Local police are on standby and have been instructed not to interfere. We've located her vehicle and placed a tracker on it in case it gets that far. I'm working on another option. You'll know it when you see it. Don't hesitate. Now say something so she doesn't think we're formulating a plan."

"I don't care what the police chief says. This is our case, not theirs. They will follow our lead," I said, hoping I sounded convincing.

I couldn't help but wonder what Dave had up his sleeve. I hated winging it. I'd much rather have a solid plan in place, but I didn't have much of a choice in that instance. I trusted my team with my life, and I hoped with every breath of my being that they didn't let me down.

Once the duffel bags were filled with cash, Pamela gestured from me to the bags. Reluctantly, I returned my gun to the holster on my side since I would need to carry one in each hand.

Suddenly, Pamela put both hands on the manager's chest and shoved him into the vault, slamming the door closed and locking him inside. I felt a slight bit of relief knowing he was out of harm's way.

"Let's go," she chirped and headed for the back door.

She motioned for me to move in front of her. "You go first and make sure the coast is clear. If there's a trigger-happy cop out there, I'd rather it be your head that gets blown off."

I slowly pushed the door open and poked my head out to survey the area. Cars were driving down the road, and several people were milling about here and there, but I honestly didn't see any of my team members or any other police officers around.

"Seems clear to me," I told her.

We stepped outside and walked down the sidewalk to the corner, where we waited for a break in traffic to cross the street.

I was on high alert, carefully watching everything so I didn't miss whatever Dave had planned. Because I knew I couldn't get in the car with her if I wanted to live to see another day.

Suddenly, an armored truck turned onto the street and barreled toward us at a high rate of speed. As instructed, I didn't hesitate. I dropped the bags, shoved Pamela as hard as I could, and dove for cover.

Pamela's body pitched forward and collided with the front of the truck, exploding on contact. The truck rolled onto its side and slid several yards before it crashed into a concrete barrier and came to a stop.

I jumped to my feet and ran to help whoever was in the truck. I knew it was someone from my team, and I prayed they weren't seriously injured.

Hoisting myself on top of the truck, I reached for

the handle right as Dave pushed the door open. He climbed out, cradling his arm, but he had a huge grin on his face. "We got her."

"We sure fucking did," I smiled. "Are you okay?"

"Yeah, I'm okay. I think my arm might be—" His words were cut off when his body jerked, and the sound of gunfire filled the air.

I pulled my gun from my holster and turned toward the sound. Searing hot pain ripped through my shoulder, then my chest, stealing my breath from me. I managed to get two shots off before I fell to the ground, gasping for air.

17

ASPEN

The sound of a woman screaming woke me. I shot straight up in bed and frantically looked around my room, unsure of what to do. The scream was followed by gut-wrenching sobs, and it sounded like Josie.

I got out of bed and hurried to the door to see what was happening. The door pushed open before I reached it, and Coal stepped into the room.

"Coal!" I gasped in surprise and jumped into his arms, elated to see him for the first time in weeks.

But my happiness was short-lived. "Aspen," he choked out. "We have to go."

Josie's sobs were quieter, but I could still hear them in the background. That's when I noticed the devastated look on Coal's face.

"What happened?"

Coal put me down and placed his hands on my shoulders. "Luke was shot. He's alive, but it's bad. We need to get to the hospital," he said, struggling to contain his emotions.

"I can't go. I'm not supposed to leave here," I reminded him.

"You can now. Your mother's dead, and the man who was helping her is in custody," he explained.

I quickly got dressed while I tried to process the news. My mother was dead, and Luke had been shot.

"Did she shoot Luke?"

"No, her accomplice did. And then Luke shot him."

"We're leaving now!" Tatum shouted from somewhere in the house.

"We'll be right behind you," Coal said.

I waited until we were in his truck on the way to the hospital before I asked for more details. "What exactly happened?"

"I don't know everything, but from what I've been able to get, Pamela showed up at the bank with a bomb strapped to her chest. They were outside on the street when it exploded. Then, her partner shot Luke, and he returned fire."

"Who was her partner?"

"I don't know. Tatum might be able to tell us at the hospital."

When we arrived at the hospital, we were shown to a waiting room and told Luke was in surgery. Tatum had her arms around Josie, who was damn near inconsolable.

"Have you called your mom?" I asked quietly.

"Yeah, her and my dad are on their way."

"You said it was bad. How bad?"

"He was shot in the left shoulder and left upper chest," Tatum said.

"Do you know who shot him?" I asked.

"Edgar Romero."

"Romero?" I asked, surprised to hear a familiar name.

Tatum nodded. "Yes. He's the brother of Edwin Romero, the man Pamela worked for until they were arrested."

"That can't be a coincidence."

"It's not," she confirmed. "From what we've pieced together so far, Pamela started sending large amounts of money to Edgar shortly after she was released from prison. We don't know why, but we suspect she owed him money or he was blackmailing her."

"Is that why she killed her husband? For his money?"

"It looks that way. And that's probably why she came after you. Edgar has refused to say much of anything, but I'm going to see what I can do to persuade him to talk once we know more about Luke."

"Are you sure Pamela's dead?" I hated to ask, but I needed to know for my own peace of mind.

"Oh, yes. I'll tell you the details if you really want to know," she offered.

"I think I need to hear them."

Coal let go of my hand he was holding and put his arm around my shoulders, giving me his silent support.

"She had a bomb strapped to her. Luke pushed her in front of an armored truck, and the bomb went off when she was hit. There's not much left of her."

"Thank you for telling me."

I sat quietly, trying to process my emotions. It felt wrong to be relieved about the death of another person, especially when that person was my mother. But that's the only word that described how I felt. Relieved.

And then I started to feel guilty. Because the price of my relief may have been Luke's life.

Surprisingly, it was Josie who pulled me out of my spiraling thoughts. "Aspen, please don't feel guilty about this. Luke wanted to make sure you were safe, and that's what he did. He knew the risks and was still willing to take them."

I couldn't hold back my tears any longer. "I can't lose him. I was just starting to let myself love him," I admitted.

Josie left her sister and moved to my side. She pulled me against her and held me while we both cried.

When my tears finally started to subside, I looked up to see Tatum wiping her own tears and glaring at Batta. "Your spawn is making me weak."

I tried not to laugh and ended up snorting, followed by a choking sound.

"Look what you've done to Aspen," Batta said, causing the rest of us to chuckle. It was exactly what was needed to break up the heaviness of the room.

We waited for hours for news.

Kathleen and her husband arrived, as did Phoenix and Annabelle. Copper and Layla also joined us.

Finally, a doctor appeared at the door and asked for the next of kin. I took Kathleen's hand and stood. "I'm his daughter, and this is his sister."

We stepped into the hallway and waited for him to tell us about Luke.

"He's in recovery now and will be moved to intensive care. One of the bullets hit a major vessel, and he lost a lot of blood. We were able to repair it and stop the bleeding, but there's extensive damage to the area. There's a chance he could start bleeding again and will require more surgery. We're going to monitor him closely for the next twelve hours. I'm sorry. I wish I had better news to give you."

I stared at him, unsure of what to say. He was supposed to tell us the surgery went well and Luke would be okay. Instead, we were still in the same position we were in before he spoke to us—not knowing if Luke was going to make it.

"Thank you, doctor," Kathleen said. "When can we see him?"

"As soon as he's moved to his room. One of the nurses will come get you when it's time."

"What did he say?" Josie asked as soon as we returned to the waiting room.

I felt like I was in a daze and couldn't find the words to speak. Coal reached for my hand and guided me to the seat beside him while Kathleen told her what the doctor said.

Tatum got to her feet. "I'll be back," she said and left the room like a woman on a mission.

She still hadn't returned when we were shown to the ICU waiting room or when Luke was allowed to have visitors, though he could only have two at a time.

Coal and I went to see him first. I gasped at the sight of him and wished someone would've warned me about how he would look. He was unbelievably pale and covered in tubes and wires.

I reached for his hand and was shocked at how cool it felt in mine. Then, I leaned close to his ear and told him the words I should've said to him years ago. "I love you, Luke. You're the closest thing to a dad I've ever had, and I don't want to lose you. Please, please fight to stay with me." With tears rolling down my face, I placed a kiss on his cheek and stepped back so Coal could have a moment with him. I didn't want to leave him, but I knew we had to keep our visit short so everyone else could have a chance to see him.

Kathleen and Jeff went next. Then Batta went in with Josie. Once everyone had a chance to visit, I was ready to go back in and stay by his side until he was able to go home.

"Since he can only have two visitors at a time, I think we should work out a schedule. That way, someone will always be here with him, and we'll still be able to get some rest," Kathleen suggested.

We agreed and decided to split the day into eight-hour shifts with Josie on first, me on second, and Kathleen on third.

"We should probably get going so you can get some sleep before it's your turn to stay with him," Coal said when the sun started to rise. I knew he was right, but I didn't want to leave. What if something happened and I wasn't there?

As if reading my mind, Josie said, "I'll call if there are any changes."

I nodded and reluctantly left the hospital with Coal.

* * *

When I entered Luke's room for my shift, I was surprised to see Tatum in the room with Josie. "How's he doing?" I asked.

"About the same," Josie said. "His vital signs have remained stable, and there's been no sign of bleeding."

I exhaled in relief. He made it past the twelve-hour mark. "No news is good news, right?"

"Speaking of news," Tatum said and got up to close the door. "I went to see Edgar, and he was very forthcoming with information."

"Really? I thought you said he was refusing to talk."

She grinned. "He was, but it's amazing what withholding someone's pain medicine will do."

"You didn't?"

"I did what I had to do to get the job done."

"So, what did he say?" I asked.

"Where's Coal?" she asked. "I thought he'd be with you."

"He dropped me off at the front and went to park his truck. He should be here any minute."

As if on cue, the door opened, and Coal walked in.

I was dying to know what Edgar told Tatum and couldn't wait much longer. "Luke is stable. No changes. Tatum got Edgar to talk, and she was just about to tell me what he said."

Coal laughed at my impatience and took a seat. "Let's hear it."

"When Edgar's brother and Pamela were arrested years ago, they lost a lot of money. The drugs they were selling were confiscated, and he didn't have the money to get more to keep their business going. It took him years to rebuild, but he was nowhere near the level they'd been at before. When Pamela was released from jail, he felt like she owed him for what he'd lost. She married the rich guy and started making payments to Edgar. Everything was fine until her husband cut off her access to his money. She convinced Edgar to change his will and leave everything to her so she could continue paying him. That worked until the will was contested, and bodies started showing up on her property. She asked Edgar for a place to hide out until things settled down, and she got her money back. He gave her a place to stay but made her work for him in the meantime. And that's where she ultimately fucked up. He had her packaging and shipping cocaine to unoccupied residences for his distributors to pick up. I guess she thought it would be funny to use Luke's address for one of the pickups."

"Pamela was the one sending the boxes?" I asked in disbelief.

Tatum nodded. "Yep. And Edgar found out what she'd done when Sydney got arrested. Which is also how Pamela figured out you were back in Devil Springs. To save her own ass, she convinced him to help her take out a life insurance policy on you. He took Coal and gave his gun to Pamela before taking him to the cabin. She took you and used Coal's gun to shoot you. After she got rid of your car, Edgar picked her up, and they drove back to the cabin with the intention of killing Coal. They were going to make it look like a murder-suicide. But he escaped, and you lived. Well, until you didn't. You know how it turned out from there."

I stared at her in disbelief. "I don't even know what to say."

She shrugged. "There's not much to say. It's a fucked-up story."

"Do you believe him?"

"I do. There's a team on the way to search the cabin and collect evidence as we speak. We should know for sure if he's telling the truth by the end of the day."

"So, what happens now?"

"A lot of paperwork," she laughed. "When it's all said and done, Edgar will likely spend the rest of his life in prison. Carter will be cleared of his charges and will be granted his rightful inheritance. And once Luke gets better, we can tie this shitshow up with a pretty little bow and put it behind us."

"You think he's going to make it?" I asked quietly.

"Yeah, I really do."

I hoped she was right.

EPILOGUE

ASPEN

"They're on their way," Coal announced.

"Crap! I'm not ready. Will you finish these cupcakes so I can change clothes?" I asked.

"Yes, but mine aren't going to look as good as yours," he warned.

"It's fine. Just do the best you can," I said and handed him the bag of frosting.

Luke was on his way home from the hospital, and we were having a small welcome-home party for him.

Josie was adamant that he wouldn't want us to make a big fuss over him, which is likely why Tatum insisted we did. I didn't care one way or the other. I was just happy he was alive and well enough to come home. His doctors said it would take some time, but they expected him to make a full recovery.

I returned to the kitchen to find Game working on the cupcakes instead of Coal. "I watched him do two, and then I had to step in," he explained and pointed to the two cupcakes with a glob of icing on top. Then, he continued decorating the remaining cupcakes like a professional. He noticed me staring and grinned. "Don't bother asking because I won't tell you."

Any other time, I would have pushed him for answers, but at that moment, I was running out of time and grateful for his help.

"Grab the pigs in a blanket. I've got the cupcakes," I said. We hurried to the common room and placed the last two trays of food on the table seconds before they pulled into the parking lot.

I watched through the window as Josie escorted Luke to the front door. His arm was in a sling, but he seemed steady on his feet.

When they came through the door, shouts of "Surprise!" and "Welcome home!" filled the room.

He glanced at Josie and then found Tatum in the crowd. "I knew you two were up to something."

Tatum grinned. "Yes, you should have. Your skills must be slipping."

"Let the man at least come in and have a seat before you start giving him shit," Batta said.

"Where's the fun in that?"

While Josie led him to a sofa, I made my way over so I could give him a hug before he sat down. I hadn't seen him on his feet since before the shooting, and there was just something different about hugging someone when they were standing up versus sitting down.

He smiled when he saw me coming and wrapped his good arm around me when I reached him. "I suppose you had something to do with this too."

"Maybe," I confessed and let go of him so he could sit. "Do you want something to eat or drink?"

"Yes, please," he answered quickly. "You were right. Hospital food is disgusting."

"I'll get it if you'll stay with him," Josie said.

"I don't need a babysitter," Luke argued.

"Yeah, well, I need you to have one," she said over her shoulder as she left to get his food.

Luke sighed and shook his head.

"This has been hard for her," I said quietly. "Let her take care of you. I think she needs to."

"I'm trying," he admitted. "It's not something I'm used to, or comfortable with, for that matter."

"You're a tough guy. You can handle anything for a couple of weeks."

"Since when are you the one giving me pep talks?"

"Since you had to go and outdo me by getting shot twice," I teased.

"I still have you both beat," Coal said and joined us on the couch.

"We are not having a 'who can get shot the most' competition," Luke said flatly.

"Aspen, can you come here for a second?" Josie asked from the kitchen.

"I'll stay with him," Coal offered before I had a chance to ask.

EPILOGUE

COAL

"I need to make this quick before either one of them comes back."

Luke turned to me with a knowing look on his face. "You want to marry Aspen."

I nodded. "Yes, and I'd like your permission to ask her. You two can deny it all you want, but she thinks of you as her father, and you think of her as your daughter."

He smiled proudly. "I don't know if permission is the right word, but you have my blessing."

"Thank you," I said and inhaled deeply. Even though I knew she'd say yes, I was still nervous.

Luke chuckled beside me. "This party isn't for me, is it?"

"Yes and no. It was the best way to get everyone here without raising her suspicions," I explained. "I hope you're not disappointed."

"Are you kidding?" he asked incredulously. "I didn't want a party to begin with. And now that I know this one isn't really for me, I won't feel bad for leaving early.

I'm ready to lay on a mattress that isn't covered in plastic. So, I suggest you get on with it, because as soon as I eat, I'm out of here."

"I guess there's no time like the present," I said as Josie and Aspen walked toward us with a plate of food and a drink for Luke.

I took the drink from Aspen and placed it on the table beside Luke. Then, I took her hand and walked a few feet away from where he was sitting.

Dropping to one knee, I presented her with the ring I'd purchased while she was at the safe house.

"We've been through a lot over the last few weeks. I wouldn't have gotten through any of it without you, and I don't want to go through anything else without you by my side. I love you with an intensity I didn't know was possible. Will you marry me?"

"Yes! Of course, I'll marry you!" she shouted.

I stood just in time to catch her as she launched herself at me. She clung to me tightly as the room erupted in cheers.

"I love you, Coal."

"I love you, too, Aspen. Forever and always."

ABOUT THE AUTHOR

Website/Newsletter Sign-up

Facebook Reader Group

Signed Books/Merchandise

ALSO BY TEAGAN BROOKS

Blackwings MC

Dash

Duke

Phoenix

Carbon

Shaker

Badger

Blackwings MC Box Set

Blackwings MC - Devil Springs

Copper

Judge

Savior

Batta

Bronze

Bear

Coal

Game

King Mountain Shifters

Slade

Standalones

Beached

Christmas in Tinsel Town

Printed in Great Britain
by Amazon

57598809R00116